. . . and you win some

Printed in the United States of America

First Printing, 2013

ISBN 97806158664860

Moore's Publishing
P.O. Box 13772
Birmingham, AL 35202

www.thegleanse.blogspot.com

Edited by Marcus Cylar of Cylar & Cylar Consulting
        Liz Reed of Blue Rooster Press
        Kristian R. Smith, Educator

Cover Design by L. Nicole Slater

Dedication

This book is dedicated to two young men that have passed on. In their life and their death, they both inspired me to pursue my dreams.

To my big brother Corey Abasi Moore- Though your life was cut short, you made a huge impact in many people's lives. That impact continues on today through your son. I promise to always keep your memory alive.

To Anthony J. Riley, T. Riley is what we called him- Look at ya' girl, A. Mo. I got my hands on the keyboard and I'm in charge!

I love and miss you both!

A Writer's Prayer

Lord, keep me off the page.

When I write, I come before You, desiring for my life and those of others to be altered through You, in spite of my human imperfections. Keep me from putting words together that only sound nice but make no real impact and require no real sacrifice on my part. God forbid, I rely on my talent instead of You. I pray I will not soak up Your praise, become puffed up with pride, or print things just to receive the world's admiration. Thank You for trusting me with a gift that affords me the opportunity to reach the hearts of Your people.

To God be the glory.

. . . and you win some

Alison S. Moore

Wynsome Olivet hovered over the bookstore shelves looking for all fifteen books she needed for her twelve-hour class load. Her parents urged her to buy used books but she could not understand their reasoning. Being the only girl and the youngest child, she had always been spoiled by her family. All of a sudden, they wanted to teach her to be thrifty. She never had to worry about cost before. They knew good and well Wynsome didn't do used and wasn't interested in sharing—not her car, not her clothes, and especially not her man. She had even scored the most coveted asset in college—a private dorm room. The older man serving as the director of student housing just couldn't resist her charm.

Wynsome finally laid eyes on one of the sociology books she needed, the last copy available. When she bent over to grab it off the bottom shelf, a short Asian guy reached for it at the same time. When he had the book firmly in his grasp, he pulled it close to his stout body. Wynsome rolled her eyes in annoyance.

"Hi. I'm Brian. What's your name?"

"Pissed." With a deep sigh, Wynsome continued, "May I have that book, please?" Wynsome said with her outstretched hand in his face.

"How 'bout we make a trade? I'll hand over the book, and you give me your phone number."

Wynsome moved so close to Brian their noses almost touched. He could smell the butterscotch candy on her breath. They were both the same five feet, five inch frame. With her sweetest smile, she tugged at the few whiskers on his chin with her right hand and leaned in to whisper in his left ear.

"Is that a fair trade?" Wynsome quizzed as she slipped the book out of his hand with her left.

"Um hmm," Brian moaned, completely under her spell.

"You may have the privilege of watching me walk away, but that's about all you can have," she said. Wynsome smoothly pivoted her sandaled feet and sauntered to the checkout line. *"Poor child, don't even know what hit 'em,"* Wynsome thought.

Brian didn't object. He was too focused on watching her walk away. He wasn't afraid to admit that he admired the curves on African American women. Brian was mesmerized by her long black hair, petite waist, and ample bottom. A group of guys walked by, amused by Brian's hypnotized state and slacked jaw.

"Don't feel bad, man. She's a notorious man-eater," one of the guys bellowed as he and his boys stepped in line. Three students separated them from Wynsome's lovely backside.

"What are you talking about?" Brian asked with one eyebrow raised.

"The girl you were talking to, Wynsome. Man, Hall & Oates didn't lie."

"Hall & Oates?" all the other guys exclaimed in harmony with puzzled expressions on their faces.

"Yeah, Hall & Oates! The beauty is there, but a beast is in the heart."

"You guys look like upperclassmen and she's a freshman. How do you know all this stuff about her?"

The Hall & Oates fan answered, "Word gets around, man. Me and Wynsome went to the same high school. It's something about that girl. She must have some kind of magical powers; like voodoo."

One of the other guys chimed in, "She does have relatives in New Orleans. I grew up in the same neighborhood with her. My little brother even took her to the prom. She left him dazed, the same way she left you standing in the middle of this bookstore," he concluded, inciting laughter from the rest of the guys.

~~~

After he left the bookstore, Brian took his newly purchased books to his dorm room. When he opened the door to Suite 115, he found a book bag laying on the very bed he had chosen for himself. Before he had time to get wound up about it, he noticed a sound coming from the bathroom.

While he sat on the opposite bed waiting for his apparent suitemate to emerge, Brian envisioned all the fun they were destined to have in Suite 115. The four-person suite included two vertical bedrooms the size of his mother's standard-sized walk-in closet. From his open door, he could see the only bathroom seated next to the kitchen on the right. The kitchen was kind of small but it probably wouldn't get much use other than keeping beer cold and housing leftover pizza. The furniture in the common area directly across from the kitchen looked like it came from a moderate-priced hotel lobby. The weird setup reminded Brian of the cross that dangled from his grandmother's rosary beads.

Impatient, Brian walked to the bathroom door and rapidly knocked, eager to find out who was behind it. A timid "yes" seeped through the whitewashed door.

"Are you okay? You've been in there for a while," Brian asked.

"Oh. I'm fine. Do you need to get in here?"

"No. Who are you? What's your name, I mean?

Brian's suitemate rushed to pull his pants up and flush the toilet. He quickly opened the door and found Brian standing entirely too close.

"I'm Daniel, nice to meet you!" Daniel held his hand out in greeting. Brian looked down at Daniel's hand with one eyebrow raised and said, "You may want to wash that first."

Daniel nodded and moved toward the sink outside the bathroom to the left. A perfect setup so that one guy could start getting ready while another one took a shower. *Goodbye to the little bit of peace, quiet, and solitude I will get in college,* Daniel thought to himself.

4

~~~

That night, Wynsome strolled around campus with Clarissa, one of her dorm mates. She insisted on coming to the party with her. Wynsome reluctantly agreed even though she preferred to ride solo. She did not get along with other females because jealousy and envy always seemed to infiltrate those kinds of relationships. She got along better with men.

The Office of Campus Life gave the incoming freshman an authentic-looking luau complete with a roasted pig. Plush green grass, tall broad trees, and brick walls protected the campus from the deteriorating neighborhoods surrounding it.

Wynsome's companion talked a mile a minute about her hometown, irritating the hell out of her. She tried to think of a polite way to tell her to shut up, but a group of guys by the administration building caught her attention. Unfortunately, the annoying guy from the bookstore stood among them. Wynsome saw Clarissa was checking them out too. She decidedly laid down her intentions.

"He is good looking, isn't he?" Wynsome said.

"Who?" Clarissa replied embarrassed that she got caught looking.

Looking in the direction of the guys, Wynsome said "I'm talking about the tall one leaning on the stair rail. I know you noticed him."

"Oh, he just reminds me of someone from back home, that's all," Clarissa responded, her face turning as red as her candy apple lipstick.

"I don't normally go for guys who aren't in shape. But even though he is a little plump, I must admit his rugged face and tree trunk arms are appealing. Yeah, I think I'll take him for myself," Wynsome added.

Suddenly gaining a voice, Clarissa said, "Well that's pretty siddity of you to say. What if you're not his type?"

Amused, Wynsome responded, "I'm everyone's type. All I have to do is strategically place myself in his line of sight, and I know he will take care of the rest."

The young men by the administration building stood enjoying the sight of beautiful coeds blanketing the lawn and dressed in colorful flowing dresses with matching leis and flowers in their hair. Some girls were in their regular street clothes, but most took advantage of the occasion. The guys were satisfied with just the leis that were given out at the entrance of the party. *These same girls will be sitting next to me in class on Monday.* That thought brought a devilish grin to Daniel's face.

Daniel nudged Brian, "You see the short girl in the long blue dress?"

The sight of her distracted Daniel from his bewildered state. He had been contemplating all the things they had discussed in freshman orientation, and millions of questions ran through his head. *How many credits to take? Did I pick the right major? Which extracurricular activities to get involved in?* The questions could go on forever.

"You mean the one talking to the girl who needs a tan?" Brian asked. Daniel couldn't get enough of Brian's often-amusing, straightforward commentary.

"Don't waste your time thinking about her," Brian stated. "I already tried talking to her in the campus bookstore. Can you believe how much books are? I thought I was going to have money to blow from the stipend that my temple back home gave me but it is not even enough for books!"

"You're Jewish?" Daniel asked in awe.

"No, no, no. Not a Jewish temple, Baha'i temple. My mom was raised Catholic, but she went through this enlightenment period where she discovered the oneness of God," Brian explained off-handedly. "Weird for a boy raised in the South, I know," he added with a shrug.

"Oh," was all Daniel could think to say.

Their other suitemates stood next to them. Burke and Ernest had the court advantage in Suite 115. Both from Pennsylvania, they had been best friends since their first day of kindergarten at Triune Christian Academy.

When Daniel met them earlier in the day, he couldn't help but think of the Sesame Street characters, Bert and Ernie. Not only did their names resemble the puppets' but their heights as well. Ernest was about three-fourths the height of Burke's six-feet-nine-inch frame. Both were clean-cut, blue-eyed, and blonde, but Ernest wasn't quite as charismatic as Burke.

"Brian, I think you've gotten off track." Ernest said trying to redirect Brian back to the original conversation.

"Oh yeah, I tried talking to her in the bookstore, but she completely blew me off. Wynsome is her name. What kind of name is that? It's not a name, I tell 'ya. It's the sound my little brother makes when he sneezes. She is a sassy one, though. I had to hold in a laugh when she told me her name was 'Pissed,' but she still thinks too highly of herself."

"Maybe she just doesn't think too highly of you," Burke teased.

Daniel separated from the fellas and walked confidently in her direction. Not wanting to miss the action, all his suitemates galloped behind him.

Ernest was the first one to reach her. Wynsome's dorm mate hesitantly walked off when they approached. It's no way she could compete with Wynsome.

"What's up? I'm Ernest. These are my suitemates—Burke, Brian, and Daniel. "Wynsome looked at Brian and said, "Didn't we meet earlier today?"

"Yes. . .we did," Brian stammered.

"Yeah, when we were standing over there, he said he thought he recognized you. You have a unique name," Ernest said.

"Yeah. You don't run into many Wynsomes," she replied.

"Oh, that is different but I thought you said her name was 'Pissed?'" Ernest said as he gave Brian an intense stare. Brian laughed sheepishly and Wynsome joined in. They all ended up on the promenade and engaged in a lengthy let-me-get-to-know-you conversation. Wynsome was the only female surrounded by four attractive men. Just the way she liked it.

~~~

Daniel hunted in his walk-in closet for something to wear on his first date with Wynsome. He couldn't believe a girl like her agreed to let him take her out. After much deliberation, he finally settled on a dark blue wash pair of jeans, a button down striped polo, and all-white Air Force Ones. *Look at that face with a fresh new cut and shave,* Daniel thought as he checked himself out in his full-length mirror. Making sure he had Wynsome's home address saved in his phone, he dashed down the steps that emptied onto the first floor of his parent's house, dividing the kitchen from the living room.

When Daniel pulled up, he spotted Wynsome peeking out the plantation shutters in her parents' living room. Even though they both had already moved their belongings into their dorm rooms, they were spending one last weekend at home with their families who weren't ready to let them go yet.

As he pulled into her driveway, a black sedan backed out almost side-swiping him. That must be her aunt taking Wynsome's grandmother back to the assisted living facility. Wynsome had told Daniel her grandmother visited on Saturdays. She had a very close-knit family who spent a lot of time together. When Wynsome noticed an unknown car pull in the driveway, she thought, *Oh shit, I hope he didn't see me in the window. I haven't been this excited about a boy since high school, but high school was just a few months ago. I can't let on that I'm excited to see him.*

Wynsome's brother, Bruce, yelled from the kitchen, "He hasn't stood you up has he Wyni? This boy isn't starting out on the good foot by being late for the first date."

"He just pulled up." Wynsome responded as she joined the family at the kitchen table.

"That's the doorbell," Wynsome said. "Bruce, you answer it. No, no. That's okay. I'll get it. You stay right where you are. I don't want you embarrassing the family name."

When she opened the door, Daniel stood there with two bouquets of flowers, both lilies.

"These are for you," he said, giving her a hug.

"Oh, thanks, Daniel. You are so sweet. These are my favorite, too."

With contrived shock, Daniel replied "Really?" not letting on that he knew from his internet search. That would come off as stalker-ish.

"Let me introduce you to everyone. My grandmother and aunt just left. "Mom, Dad, Bruce, I'd like you to meet Daniel Roberts. Daniel, this is my father, my mother, and my older brother Bruce. Bruce may try, but please don't let him intimidate you."

"Nice to meet you," Wynsome's mom said. "Would you like to sit down for some chocolate cake before you all head out on your date?"

"No ma'am. I don't want to impose," Daniel responded.

"Boy, where are you from? Don't you know it's rude to refuse food in a southern household, or don't you have any home training?" Bruce growled.

Before Daniel had a chance to respond, Wynsome went in for the save, "Mom, we should get going before the place gets too crowded anyway."

Looking confused and a little shaken, Daniel handed Mrs. Olivet the second bouquet of flowers. "These are for you."

"Oh, Daniel, these are beautiful," she exclaimed giving Daniel a big hug.

"Where are you young people going anyway?" Wynsome's dad chimed in.

"I thought it would be fun for us to do some roller skating, laser tag, and putt-putt golf," Daniel said looking at Wynsome for her approval.

"You don't know my daughter very well. She doesn't like to play children's games." Wynsome's dad said.

Wynsome interrupted him. "That sounds like a great idea, Daniel. I've never done any of that on a date before. It will be a new experience for me. We should get going," Wynsome said giving her father a "don't say another word look."

~~~

As Daniel watched Wynsome having trouble lacing up her skates, he cupped his hands over his eyes and whispered, "peek-a-boo." Finishing her task, Wynsome laughed trying to mask her annoyance at his silliness.

"I didn't take you to be a playful guy."

"Do I come off as too serious?" Daniel said as he carefully pulled her to her feet and guided her onto the skating rink. On the ride over, Wynsome had confessed she'd only been skating a few times in her life. She hadn't skated since Biggie Smalls died.

Wynsome shrugged, "Not too serious, but intense, I would say."

After skating for about twenty minutes, Daniel decided to bust out his best moves for Wynsome. He let go of Wynsome's hand and tried to glide his 200 pound, six-feet-tall frame on the roller rink. Trying to get Wynsome to join in, they both fell on their behinds, panting. They pulled themselves off the floor using the rail surrounding the rink for support.

"Let's take a break and get something to eat," Daniel suggested.

As they sat down to dig into their nachos with extra cheese and jalapeños, Daniel looked at Wynsome with a smirk on his face.

"What?" Wynsome asked wiping some stray cheese from the corner of her mouth.

"Nothing. It's just good to see a girl not afraid to eat and get messy on a date. This isn't exactly 'proper date food.'"

"Boy, please. I can get down with the best of them and still keep my sexy, Wynsome retorted.

She went on to ask, "How did you end up at Agee-Gadsden University?"

"It was my only choice. The only school I applied to," Daniel answered.

"Why?"

"I'm the only child, so I didn't want to go too far from home. I get to stay close to my parents and stay involved in my church. I worked my butt off to get here, too. I'm not a naturally good student. I had to study hard. What about you?"

"They had recruiters at my school's college fair. You do know I'm a graduate of the Art School of the South, music major," Wynsome emphasized sitting up straight with pride.

Bowing his head in reverence, "I am aware."

"Aren't you a little old for your parents to make you go to church?" Wynsome added, puzzled that he was so into church.

"Yeah, I am definitely too old for that. I go on my own. I actually enjoy it. My parents used to make me go but when I turned eleven they gave me the freedom to explore other beliefs."

"Hmmm, "Wynsome murmured, but let the conversation stall out. *I don't know why he is pretending to be all holy. I'm not like other girls in the South that like to play all virginal. We don't have to play that game,* Wynsome thought.

After finishing their nachos and sodas, they chose putt-putt golf as their next event. It was a beautiful clear night with a perfect summer breeze. After getting their clubs and balls, Wynsome continued to quiz Daniel.

"So, after your parents gave you a choice and allowed you to explore, you still chose to be a Christian?"

"Uh huh."

"Even with the Christian's antiquated stance on sex?"

"I'll have to tell you more about that some other time. I have to get to know you a little better first," Daniel said with a teasing grin.

"Don't try to change the subject now," Wynsome said.

"I ain't scared," Daniel replied. "I think people focus too much on what you can't do as a Christian. That's not the point. Sex is a good thing. God created it for us to enjoy; it's the world that has perverted its purpose."

Amazed, Wynsome said, "I didn't think you church types were open-minded like that. "

Daniel laughed, "Oh, but we aren't church types. My parents taught me what it meant to have a personal relationship with Christ, and I decided to serve Him on my own. I really got to know Him for myself."

Contemplatively, Wynsome said, "I wasn't raised going to church. I guess that makes me a heathen, huh?"

Since Wynsome seemed to be more interested in talking than playing golf, Daniel found a bench and started walking towards it. When he sat down, he motioned for her to join him.

"I don't think you are a heathen. What is a heathen anyway?" Daniel asked.

"I'm just joking. Seriously, though, how do you feel about people who think differently than you?

"I do believe Jesus is the only way, but I don't have any problem with anyone who doesn't agree. Let me be free to believe what I believe, and I'll let you be free to disagree."

"My parents raised me to just be a good person and to work hard," Wynsome shared. "My dad is very turned off by organized religion. My mom wanted us to go to church, but my dad was so against it, Mom stopped trying. He said the church was full of hypocrites raising hell."

"Do you know what happened to make your dad feel that way?"

"It's a pretty sad story," Wynsome said hesitantly, but Daniel gave her a look that said she could feel safe to continue. "My father had been a foster child since he was three years old. When he turned ten, the system finally found a family that would take him in long term."

"Wow. I couldn't imagine what it must feel like to not have a family. My family is everything to me," Daniel said.

"It has affected my dad a great deal. He doesn't like to talk about his experience in foster care. He'd rather forget about it. But when he stayed with this particular family, he developed a very close relationship with his foster brother, and they stayed friends even after they had families of their own. He was like an uncle to me and Bruce," Wynsome said.

"So what happened to change everything?" Daniel inquired.

"Out the blue, my uncle's wife left him and took their five year old son with her. She cut off all communication from their family and friends. My uncle was so sad that he couldn't see his son, my dad let Bruce hang out with him to try to fill the void. Eventually it all came out that Uncle's wife left because he was sexually abusing their son. Uncle was a DJ at the Christian radio station. He was so influential to my dad, my dad was starting to think about joining his church."

"Did your uncle. . . ever do anything to your brother?" Daniel asked.

"Thankfully, no, "Wynsome replied. "At least that is what Bruce has said but my mom thinks he may be suppressing something. My mom wanted Bruce to go get counseling but my dad didn't think it was necessary."

Not knowing exactly what to say, Daniel stated. There are some sick people in this world. My parents didn't grow up in the church. They got to know Christ while dating each other. I can definitely understand where your dad is coming from. That's why I love Jesus — he's nothing like us. He's not shady." That's why we need Him."

"He may not be shady, but he let these shady characters get away with shit, excuse my language. Is your daddy a preacher?" Wynsome asked but didn't give Daniel a chance to respond. "This conversation is too deep for a first date," she concluded.

In a gentler tone, Wynsome stared at Daniel with a mix of admiration and perplexity, "You certainly are a different kind of guy," She hadn't yet figured out what to make of him.

"Why don't you come to church with me and my family tomorrow?"

"Uh, I don't know about that," Wynsome said apprehensively.

"Aww. Come on."

"We'll see. I won't make any promises though."

II

When Daniel made it back to his parent's house, the first thing he did was knock on his parents' door to say good night. His mom, Carol, lay in bed next to her husband of twenty-five years, absent-mindedly flipping through channels. After Daniel left the room, she continued her futile attempt to relax and veg out on TV. *It's a shame you can't find interesting, meaningless programs out of a thousand channels,* Carol thought, finally settling on CNN.

"Paul, look at that handsome Anderson Cooper," she said. "He is so intelligent but down to earth. He can switch from talking about the economic crisis to the latest episode of *The Real Housewives of Atlanta* in the blink of an eye. You know, he loves that show."

Not paying Carol much attention, Paul nodded slightly as he continued to focus on the paperwork in his lap.

"Honey, bed is for bedtime, not work," Carol huffed.

"I'm sorry, sweetheart. Can I get a pass this one time? You know my department is up for reaccreditation. I need to make sure we are more than prepared." Paul chaired the communication arts department at the University, and Carol served as coordinator for the at-risk program in the county school system. They both started thirty years ago as elementary school teachers in the city schools. Their passion for education brought them together then, but Carol didn't appreciate the University interfering with her quality time right now. She looked toward the heavens and thought, *this is an opportunity for me to exercise some of that longsuffering the Bible talks about.*

Trying to distract her husband, Carol leaned over and kissed his nose, pulled the paperwork out of his hand and placed it on the nightstand on her side of the bed so they could snuggle. Paul wrapped her in his arms, lessening the divide even further. "Are you feeling neglected?" Paul asked playfully as he nibbled on her ear and neck.

"Yes," Carol purred.

"Well, I'll make it up to you Monday night after Daniel officially moves on campus. We can stay right here at home, and I'll cook your favorite pork roast with grilled asparagus and a nice salad. And no meal would be complete without my famous sweet potato cheesecake!" Paul offered.

"That's a great idea, sweetheart. We can spend quality time at home together but right now, can I have more of those kisses?" Carol asked as she guided her husband on top of her.

~~~

"Dad, Mom is really anxious. Could you please come down for breakfast before she blows a blood vessel?"

"Sure, son, I'm on my way."

Paul's six-feet-five frame followed Daniel's six-foot frame down the wooden staircase into the country-style kitchen where Carol had breakfast piping hot on the table. Paul savored the smell of smoked sausage, bacon, scrambled eggs, grits, and homemade biscuits.

"Eat up, we don't have much time," Carol instructed, "Hopefully, we will make it to church before praise and worship. Y'all know I hate to miss praise and worship. It throws the whole service off for me."

When the Roberts pulled up in the church parking lot, it was about thirty minutes before the service was scheduled to start. They were lucky to be alive after Carol's 'Ricky Bobby' driving demonstration. Daniel thought the car was going to turn over when his mom made that last sharp turn. Daniel noticed his cousin Michelle and her son Miller going toward the children's church enclave, but the view of Wynsome's pale green Volkswagen Jetta coming up the drive quickly sidetracked him.

When Wynsome put her car in park, Daniel opened her car door. "Good morning, how are you? Daniel greeted her.

"Just peachy, how are you?"

"I'm good. I'm so glad to see you."

As Carol and Paul walked toward the church, they heard Oneilia Sutton, the church secretary, belt out, "Good morning, God's favorite people!" as she gave them a huge hug. The Suttons were Carol's favorite couple at church. They shared the same heart for the same causes.

Carol responded, "Good morning. Have you gotten a chance to rest since the seasoned seniors' celebration Friday night?"

"We sure did, Carol; I slept all day Saturday," Ralph explained. Ralph and Oneilia were founding members of their church.

"Paul, we should get our propers for showing the womenfolk how it's done in the kitchen. We are the reason the seasoned seniors' celebration was a success," Ralph declared. Paul nodded his head and waved his right hand in agreement.

Jodie, the Suttons' only child, looked impeccable standing next to her parents. Carol couldn't help but notice the real pearl accessories in her ears, on her neck and on her wrist. She even had on make-up for a change. Carol always thought it ideal for Daniel and Jodie to get married, even though Jodie was four years older than Daniel. Who's to say, it could still happen. *I'm not too sure about this Wynsome child*, Carol thought.

"Jodie, you look flawless in that pearl suit," Carol complimented her, approving of the skirt with the perfect hem-line, a touch above the knee.

"Thank you, Mrs. Roberts," Jodie replied with the sincerest smile she could muster. She really wasn't in the mood to be social.

Jodie had so many thoughts running through her mind. She couldn't stop thinking about the mess her life had become.

"Honey, those stunning red shoes look too expensive to even touch the ground! Five-inches! I used to be able to wear shoes like that!" Carol went on, noticing Jodie's hands fidgeting around her neck.

Jodie wondered whether the bruise on the left side of her neck was noticeable. She had tried to hide it with the collar of her suit but wasn't sure she had been successful. Even though she hated wearing make-up, she wore it today to conceal the mark under her left eye.

The Suttons headed toward the church doors and motioned for the Roberts to come along, but they chose to wait on Daniel and Wynsome. When Wynsome and Daniel joined his parents at the side doors of the church, there was no time to spare. Daniel quickly introduced his crush to his parents. Paul nodded and rushed them through the doors, "Let's all get to our seats."

All church members knew where the Roberts sat. Their name was not on the pew, but it was permanently etched in the mind's eye of the congregation and any church member would take the initiative to inform any visitor who wasn't aware. They got to their usual place on the right side of the pulpit just as Michelle returned from dropping Miller off at the children's church enclave. Carol was overjoyed her niece had agreed to come to church and bring her son with her.

The praise and worship team emerged from the side doors of the sanctuary singing about the goodness of the Lord. They swayed from side to side in their color coordinated outfits declaring God's blessings throughout the city, on the job, essentially wherever we go. Carol loved this song because it reminded her that the devil is defeated and she has been released from all strongholds even sickness and poverty. Michelle enjoyed the music but didn't know exactly what to do with her limbs. She had always felt uncomfortable during praise and worship, all the raised hands and rocking back and forth. *What is all the fuss about? It don't take all that.*

Wynsome, on the other hand, was experiencing sensory overload. The band's electric guitar, saxophone, trumpet, and snare drum made her want to dance. She had to stop herself from taking it to the club.

In the rear of the church, Jodie tried hard to hide her boredom. Worship was not enjoyable for her anymore. It had become a chore. She noticed Patrick, an old acquaintance, staring at her from the opposite side of the church and said a silent prayer he would stop. Grunting, she whispered to herself, *another horrible mistake*. When her mom nudged her, she immediately started singing and clapping her hands though half-heartedly.

The Reverend Josephine Ashley, the new associate minister, moved toward the pulpit, "Good Morning, Saints!" Even though some parishioners continued to stand and worship, the choir members took their seats. "In the next two Wednesdays, we will have our first Truthseeker's Young Adult forum for ages 18-35, led by me. This is not 'yo' mama's Bible study' so please, young people, come out."

Rev. Ashley had been trying to make some major changes in the programming at the church and she hoped this one would get more young people involved and desiring to serve God. Her description intrigued Daniel and he made a mental note to attend. *I hope I can convince Michelle and Wynsome to come too.*

After Rev. Ashley took her seat, Pastor Longhorn moved toward the pulpit for his weekly message. "Good Morning, Church." Brother Odell King responded loudly from the far recesses of the church, "Mo'ning, Mo'ning," in his familiar southern drawl. Brother King was well known for responding to Pastor in the most unusual of ways. At any point during the service, he might yell "shut up," "sho' nuff," "trying to get to heaven," or "I swone it," his way of saying I swear. The teenagers cast lots to predict what he would say next. His-five-feet-five inch-stature, potbelly, and baby hands added to his caricature-like persona.

Brother King was normally the first person at church and the last one to leave. After all, when he was out in the world, he was always the first person in the shot house and the last one out, so he brought that same mentality to the Lord's house.

"This morning, I would like to take a few minutes to start a new series," Pastor Longhorn begun. "This is especially for our college students going off to school. But don't you grown folks stop listening. The Lord has something in this message for you today, too."

"For you all taking notes — and all of you should be taking notes — the title of today's lesson is 'New Beginnings.' Look to your neighbor and say 'New Beginnings.' It's a new school year, with new academic challenges, new peers, new environments, new temptations and new freedoms. Let's take some time to refocus on what our true priorities should be before getting distracted with busyness. Some of you non-students may need to make a fresh commitment to the Lord, or on your jobs, or to your spouses. Amen? "

"Our text today comes from 1 Peter 2:16 and going on to 2 Peter 1:5-11 verses. Now, remember we are talking about new beginnings and fresh commitments today. Have you all found the first scripture yet? A loud chorus of Yes could be heard all over the 1500-seat sanctuary. "Ready, read. 'Live as free men, but do not use your freedom as a cover-up for evil; live as servants of God.' College students, you will experience freedoms you have never been exposed to before. You must be prepared to make your own choices — the right choices — when your parents are not present, Amen?

"Shut up!" Brother King yelled. Wynsome looked around alarmed and confused, wondering who in the world would say that while someone is speaking. How rude! The teenagers let out a chorus of snickers from the teen corner on the left side of the pulpit.

"We like to dwell on the free men, free will part of this verse. This verse also says we should live as servants of God. How many of you can say you have been living as servants of God? Our lives are not our own, Church; we have been bought at a price. Some of us need to make a new start, a fresh start, and commit our lives back to the Lord. Some of you may be saying, 'How do we do that, Pastor?' Well lets take a look at 2 Peter 1: 5-11. I will read for your hearing. Now, pay close attention:

> For this very reason, make every effort to supplement your faith with virtue, and virtue with knowledge, and knowledge with self-control, and self-control with steadfastness, and steadfastness with godliness, and godliness with brotherly affection, and brotherly affection with love. For if these qualities are yours and are increasing, they keep you from being ineffective or unfruitful in the knowledge of our Lord Jesus Christ. For whoever lacks these qualities is so

nearsighted that he is blind, having forgotten that he was cleansed from his former sins.

"I'm running out of time, so I'll make this brief. I know a lot of you have sending off celebrations after church today." Michelle mumbled Amen. "In my reading, the word 'self-control' stayed in my Spirit. There will be many temptations for each of us on a day-by-day basis, but we must allow the Holy Spirit to teach us self-control. When those temptations come, we must be steadfast so the world can see we are servants of God. This is how we produce fruit and effectiveness for the Lord our God.

"So young people and old people alike, don't be nearsighted. Ask the Holy Spirit to develop these qualities in you increasingly. You have the power, use it! You are servants of God, act like it! Later on in this passage, it says if you practice these qualities, you will never fall. Practice virtue, knowledge, self-control, steadfastness, godliness, brotherly affection, and love. Next week, we will focus on the first quality—virtue. Ask the Lord and he will help you, Amen?

~~~

"Pastor sure did preach today," Mr. Roberts said to his family as they stood outside the church. "Now, Daniel, you remember those words Pastor spoke, and keep them in mind when you're at the illustrious Agee-Gadsden University. It's not as good as the university where I teach, but it'll do."

"You know when Jodie, Oneilia's girl, was in college, she was the president of a large campus ministry that has chapters all over the world. Oneilia said she was always traveling to different schools in different states for different conferences. You should find a group like that on campus, Daniel," Carol told her son.

"Okay, Mom. Dad, you and mom have raised me right. When I get to school, I won't forget my home training."

"Jodie also finished college a semester early and had a position waiting for her at Southern Traditions. She's even entertaining the idea of going to law school. Remember, we are on the four-year plan. The first four years are on us, anything else is on you," Carol added.

Paul jumped in, "Where would you like to go for your celebration, Daniel?"

"I have a taste for seafood. Let's go to that seafood place off of Lakeshore."

"Seafood it is," Carol said.

"Michelle, did you invite Miller's dad to lunch?" Daniel asked.

"Yes, I did. He asked me to call him when we decided on a place. I'll call as soon as we get in the car. He should be able to make it there at the same time we do."

Even though Xavier and Michelle no longer dated, they were still good friends, and Daniel had developed a special relationship with him.

Mr. Roberts directed his attention to Wynsome, "Did you enjoy the service?"

"It was great. Everyone was so welcoming," she answered.

Carol added, "We are so glad you enjoyed it. I hope you will keep coming back. Would you like to join us for lunch?"

"I would love to, but I can't today. My grandmother and my mom are cooking a huge meal for me. It was nice meeting all of you, and I look forward to seeing you again soon."

~~~

Xavier entered the restaurant right as his party was being seated. When Miller spotted his dad, he jumped into his arms and gave him a big hug around his neck. Michelle was careful to grab a seat next to Daniel. She planned to share some cautionary words with him before he began his college career. Though Michelle never attended college, she still knew what it was like to be young and dumb. When her mom died of a sudden heart attack when she was sixteen, Michelle lived with the Roberts. Her dad couldn't take care of her because he stayed on the road as a commercial truck driver. She chose not to go to college and pursued a real estate license instead. Not too long after getting her license, Michelle had her son and named him Miller, her mom's maiden name. Since her mom's death, Michelle had been more like Carol and Paul's daughter rather than just a niece.

"It's good to see you, young man. I'm sorry you couldn't join us for morning worship," Mr. Roberts said to Xavier.

After Xavier exchanged greetings with everyone and took his seat, he answered Mr. Roberts, just as the server appeared to take their drink orders.

"You know I'm a believer, Mr. Roberts. I don't have to be a member of a church in order to prove it. My relationship with God is personal. I don't have to prove it by going to church on Sunday morning. I express it in my everyday life."

"How exactly do you exhibit this relationship in your everyday life, Xavier?" Mr. Roberts asked.

Mrs. Roberts quickly changed the subject. Xavier and Paul had this same conversation every time they saw each other and Carol did not feel like hearing it again. She just wanted to have a relaxing lunch with her baby boy before he started his college career.

"So, Xavier," Carol asked, "how are the other children doing?"

"They are doing very well. Korynne and I went roller-skating in the park this morning. I just dropped her off at my ex-mother-in-law's house so I could come see Daniel off to college," he said as he rubbed Daniel's head and gave him a playful punch in the shoulder.

"Aw, man, I wanted to go," Miller whined.

"We will do something else, buddy; just me and you," Xavier assured Miller.

"Back to my original question," Mr. Roberts insisted, "how exactly do you show in your everyday life you have a relationship with Christ?"

"I treat people right. I obey the laws of the land. And I pray every day, in my own special way."

"How often do you read The Word?"

"I don't put much faith in that ancient book. I don't believe God wants us to follow it like a rulebook, but more so see it as a history book. Times have changed so much since that book was written, there's no way we could still live that way today. We are all flawed human beings, right? Flawed human beings wrote the Bible. What about the Dead Sea scrolls? I'd like to see all of those."

"Do you actually think there is something in them that will refute Jesus is God's son, who died on the cross for our sins, rose again, and is now seated in heaven right now interceding on our behalf?"

"It's something in there they don't want us to see."

"Who are "they?" It's nothing in there that will change who God is. As I have told you before, fellowshipping with other believers is very important. It helps us to sharpen one another and stay on the right track."

"It's nothing but hypocrites and liars in the church, Mr. Roberts."

"Just promise me one thing, son."

"What's that?"

"Promise me you will read that Bible we gave you when Miller was born. Before you read it, ask the Holy Spirit to guide you while you do. That's all I ask."

"I will definitely do that, sir."

Right on time, the server came back to collect their orders. After they all selected their entrées, Michelle started in on Daniel. "Now, Daniel, tell me again how you met the young lady who attended church with us today."

"Oh, here we go! Her name is Wynsome and we met during freshmen orientation. She caught my eye during the luau. She's from Birmingham, too, and she's studying music education. I really like her a lot, 'Chelle. She's beautiful, strong-willed, intelligent, and talented." Changing the subject, Daniel asked Michelle what she thought about the Bible study Rev. Ashley announced in service.

"I didn't think about it at all," Michelle said.

"Well, I'm interested in seeing how it's going to be different than all the other Bible studies we've been to. Come check it out with me," Daniel insisted with a huge grin on his face.

"I'll think about it," Michelle told Daniel, brushing him off. "Cousin," Michelle added, "Don't try to get the attention off of you. You sound like you're in love already. Don't get carried away. You were raised in a good home with a good example, so I know you know how to honor a lady with respect. Now many young men your age don't do that, so don't let your peers talk you out of what you already know to be true." In a whisper, Michelle continued, "I know your parents made you go through that True Love Waits nonsense. But you are a young man, and I know you already have urges."

"Michelle," Daniel whispered back, "I *do not* want to have this conversation with you."

"Danny, this is important. I have a package for you in Xavier's car. Always keep it with you, just in case the temptation gets too much for you. You don't want to end up in the situation I did. Miller is wonderful, but his arrival made my life much more complicated way too soon."

"I appreciate your concern, Michelle, but I plan on keeping the commitment I made to myself, and most importantly to God. Anyway, sex is too much of a distraction right now. Trust me, Cuz, me and God have this under control."

Though Paul pretended to listen to every word Carol and Xavier were saying, he was actually listening to Michelle's conversation with Daniel. His chest swelled with pride because he realized his boy knew how to stand his ground. *He really has ingested the values we tried to instill in him.*

Since she moved back to Birmingham after graduation, Jodie decided to explore her interest in music. She took the initiative to sign up for a music production class so she wouldn't get in trouble, and by trouble she meant men, men like Patrick at church.

Almost all of her childhood friends had moved away, leaving her with no social circle. Well, there was her co-worker Emberli, but she didn't have much time to hang out because she was pre-occupied nurturing her new small business after their regular day-job hours.

Instead of staying out of trouble, Jodie had a feeling she was about to run smack into it. She wavered between calling and not calling this guy, Amir, she met in the music production class. After Amir discovered Jodie also had an interest in film and editing, he gave her his business card. He insisted she call him if she was interested in learning her way around a movie camera and an editing bay. Jodie was bored and lonely so having him over would give her something to occupy her time. She finally decided to call, and they arranged for her to meet him at his house later on that day for a private lesson.

When Amir opened his back door, he led her to his second bathroom that he converted into a makeshift studio. He had expensive equipment all over the place— professional-grade video cameras, microphones, mixing boards and the like. Oddly, he had a Bible sitting on the floor on top of an empty cardboard box next to the production board. Maybe he prayed and meditated on scripture before each session for the Holy Spirit to inspire his lyrics. Emberli told her later she should just be glad he owned one.

Jodie didn't learn too much about music production or film editing that night because she was too busy removing his hands from inappropriate places. *What kind of girl does he think I am? I mean, I'm attracted to him, but I don't do that kind of thing on the first date; maybe the second, but not the first.*

~~~

Rev. Ashley sat in the young adult Sunday school classroom with nervous anticipation as she watched the young people enter the first Truthseekers Bible Study. It excited her to imagine all the ways God would move among the young people.

Daniel had managed to get Wynsome, Michelle, and Xavier to come with him. Thank God, Xavier had showed up. It looked like Daniel and he were going to be the only guys in attendance. Wynsome's brother, Bruce, was supposed to come but bailed at the last minute. Daniel spotted Jodie sitting close to the door with her interesting, to say the least, friend Emberli beside her. One of Jodie's hands tightly clutched what looked like a piece of tissue. Every time Daniel had seen her lately, she looked like she would much rather be somewhere else.

After she waited in vain for others to show, Rev. Ashley called everyone away from the refreshment table to sit in the semi-circle. "I am so glad you all decided to attend the first Truthseekers. It is my desire we will grow spiritually, collectively, and individually as we discover, accept, and act out our God-given purpose."

Oh, great! The Purpose Driven Church, The Purpose Driven Life. Yea, that hasn't been done before. Every church all over the world has studied the Rick Warren franchise. I thought this was supposed to be different from my mama's Bible study. This is going to be a waste of time, Jodie thought angrily.

"I am excited and apprehensive about this meeting. I remember being your age, and I didn't want to hear anything anyone my age had to say. My father, Deacon Rueben Rouser. . ." An 'ooh' of familiarity flew out of Michelle's mouth before she had a chance to contain it. Rev. Ashley acknowledged Michelle's expression with a nod.

"Deacon Rouser grew up in this church. He started bringing me here when I was two years old. My parents were teens when they had me. When their relationship didn't work out, my mom moved us to Nashville. I was about nine years old at the time. I ended up back here when I came to Birmingham to attend divinity school."

Daniel had to strain to hear Rev. Ashley's small voice. By appearance, you wouldn't think such a delicate tone would come from the six feet tall, rail-thin minister. She had an athletic runner's physique with her long, straight hair, pulled back into a messy ponytail. Rev. Ashley looked like she didn't take any mess from anyone!

"Now you know a little bit about me, so I'd like you all to introduce yourselves and share one thing you find difficult about being a young adult Christian. Who would like to go first?"

Xavier did not hesitate to take the lead.

"Hey, I'm Xavier. The hardest thing for me about being a young adult period is providing financially for my kids."

"Good evening. My name is Michelle, but my family calls me 'Chelle. It weighs heavily on me as a young adult to make my family proud of me."

Rev. Ashley interrupted, "I noticed neither one of you identified yourselves as a young adult Christian. Why is that?"

Xavier and Michelle started to speak at the same time. Rev. Ashley deciphered Michelle saying that it goes without saying because they were sitting in the church house. Xavier said that he didn't find a need to put labels on himself.

"It is not safe to assume that all people in the church are Christians, but that's another study for another time," Rev. Ashley replied.

Jodie tried to focus on the introductions but kept zoning out. She couldn't figure out why she had felt compelled to write Rev. Ashley a letter last night and couldn't decide whether or not to give it to her. For some reason, Jodie believed Rev. Ashley could be trusted, and Jodie hardly trusted anyone.

"I think everyone knows me. My name is Daniel. I feel my peers are watching me, waiting for me, and wanting me to fail because I'm so vocal about my relationship with Christ."

"My name is Wynsome. I'm tired of church people judging me and my family because we don't belong to a church."

"Oh, it's my turn. What's up y'all? I'm Emberli. Yea, like smoldering embers from a fire. I don't find anything difficult about being a young adult Christian. I'm good. I'm doing me."

Looking around nervously, Jodie introduced herself, "I'm Jodie. The thing I find the hardest being a young adult Christian, especially one known for growing up in the church, is people expect me to never mess up, never make mistakes, and always do everything right. That's just too much pressure."

Rev. Ashley took the floor, "I thank you all for opening up and allowing me to see a glimpse of who you are. I will be the facilitator of this group. I am not a teacher or a leader. I just guide the conversations.

Rev. Ashley led them in goal- and norm-setting so they would have a clear understanding of what they were there to do and also outline how to maintain an open, authentic, and respectful discussion.

Daniel started, "In order for this to be successful, we must agree to be as honest as possible. If we are going to be honest, then it is a must we agree everything said in here will stay in here. We can't judge each other either, y'all."

Emberli added, "I'm wit' you when you right. Off the top, we can't judge. Only God can do that. I understand it is human nature, but not in here. Leave it in your car and pick 'em back up when you get to the parking lot, if you need to."

After a brief introductory talk about her expectations for the group, Rev. Ashley closed the meeting so they could have time to fellowship with one another. Jodie noticed Rev. Ashley had slipped out the classroom after the closing remarks. She walked out trying to catch up with her. Eventually, Jodie caught up to Rev. Ashley as she exited her office with a stack of business cards in her hand.

"Jodie, were you trying to sneak out?" Rev. Ashley questioned playfully.

"No, ma'am. I was looking for you. I wanted to give you this," Jodie responded as she handed Rev. Ashley the crumbled note stained with sweat. "Please read it later when you have time. It's not urgent," Jodie added.

"You could step into my office now while I read it?" Rev. Ashley said walking towards her office without waiting for a reply.

Jodie replied, "I really have to go. Read it later. Please." Jodie bolted out the side door, giving Rev. Ashley no time to respond.

Rev. Ashley shrugged, went back into the classroom to give each young adult her business card, and then excused herself. As soon as she returned to her office, she slid off her topsiders, sat Indian style in her huge plush brown leather chair and smoothed out Jodie's letter:

> Dear Rev. Ashley,
> I usually keep all my problems to myself but I feel like I'm drowning and have no clue of what to do. Even though I have a nice house, a

career and numerous achievements, I keep making the wrong decisions. I don't know how to stop.

Sometimes I wonder if I'm even saved; saved women don't struggle with the things I struggle with. I'm supposed to know better.

J. Sutton

<div align="center">~~~</div>

Paul arrived at the church around 6:30 p.m. It was almost time for the Church Officers Board meeting. The COB charged themselves with maintaining the church's physical and spiritual structure, including spending, pastoral support, and moral leadership.

When Brother Roberts entered the conference room, all the other twelve COB members were already present and talking among themselves. It was a rare occasion for all officers to be present at the same meeting.

As soon as he entered the room, Brother Roberts called the monthly meeting to order, opened in prayer, and conducted the roll call. He passed out the minutes from the last meeting and the agenda for this meeting. "Brother Young, will you please summarize the minutes from last month for the board's approval please?"

For some unknown reason, Brother Young always rocked from side to side every time he spoke whether sitting or standing. "Yes, sir. At last month's meeting, we agreed the men's retreat would still be held the last weekend in October. We realize this is the same weekend as the Magic City Classic, and many of our members are Alabama A&M and Alabama State alumni and fans, but we are sure the true men of God would rather attend the retreat than that cesspool of debauchery."

Brother McCain thought, *I'll just do what I do every year. Leave the retreat at night and go tailgate at Legion Field with my line brothers. It's as simple as that. I'm a grown man.* He didn't look grown though. He still had the same boyish looks he had as a child and the attitude to match.

Brother Young continued, pushing his bifocals back up on his nose, "Brother Sutton suggested we include our teenagers this year. Eight out of thirteen deacons voted against it, citing the retreat has always been for adults, and there is no need to change that now. We should leave it to the teen ministry to plan a retreat for the boys. The remaining deacons opposed because they believe the young men can and need to learn Godly character with the guidance of the COB. They were outvoted."

"We also discussed the possibility of holding an AIDS Awareness workshop in December. Pastor feels God calling the church to respond to the AIDS epidemic. Yet, the motion was denied by eight out of thirteen votes because most of the deacons believe we should not sponsor such an event. It does not fit within our mission," Brother Young said with a huff.

Scrunching up his face, Brother Sutton wondered, *who are these eight deacons and how can we get rid of them?! Probably the same fools from way back when who couldn't agree on a name for the church so they just decided to name it 'Church!' Ridiculous! I'm hesitant to invite people to church because when they ask the name of it, they look at me crazy when I say Church. Forgive me, Lord for my judgmental thoughts. These are your children I'm talking about. My mama always said, 'The Lord looks out for fools and babies.'*

"Are there any additions or corrections to the minutes?" Deacon Roberts asked. The room remained quiet.

"Good. Who agrees to accept the minutes as read? Respond by saying I." Brother Rouser, Rev. Ashley's father said "I." "All opposed say 'nay.'" After a brief moment of silence, Brother Young announced, "The I's have it. I will turn the meeting back over to the chairman, Brother Roberts."

"Our first order of business is whether or not to allow unwed mothers to use the church facilities for baby showers. The Ladies Council brought this issue to our attention. We have had an increase in unwed pregnancies in the congregation. Not only is it an issue with our teenagers but with our adults as well. The Ladies Council suggested we take a stand by not allowing unwed expectant mothers to have baby showers at the church."

Brother King spoke as he stood, "Y'all just hush up. Y'all focused on the wrong thang. The problem ain't baby showers. The problem is our young people don't have a solid relationship with Christ. If they did, they would strive for holiness. What are we doing wrong as a church that our young people don't realize how important holiness is? Look, we ask Pastor to address the issue from the pulpit with a sermon on sexual purity and dismiss this nonsense about baby showers."

"Brother Ruben Rouser replied with indignation, "That mess shouldn't be discussed from the pulpit. The older members don't need to hear about that mess. Save it for the singles ministry."

"I agree with Brother King. It should be something dealt with from the pulpit. The congregation follows the lead of the pastor. And it's something every member can get from any sermon," Brother Sutton added.

Brother Rouser leaned forward and pounded on the table with his fists, "If we don't allow these fast tail girls to have baby showers at the church, it will send a message to the other girls, and maybe they will think twice about being fast."

"Calm down, Ruben. All that will do is run more young people out of the church," Brother Roberts said. "We have had enough discussion on this issue. Let's take it to a vote. All in favor of banning unwed expectant mothers from having their baby showers at the church, raise your hand." Eight of the thirteen deacons raised their hand. Brother Sutton muttered, "What a surprise."

"It is settled, Brother Roberts said, disappointed. We will not allow unwed mothers to have baby showers at the church."

"Now tell me, is the Lawd pleased?" After a long pause, Brother King exclaimed, "Y'all ain't got to say nothing!"

Everyone ignored Brother King's outburst and moved on to the next issue, the prison ministry. "We approved a motion in April that the church will respond to the crisis of our young black people being incarcerated at alarming rates by starting a prison ministry. I am proud to announce the prison ministry is up and running now. We do a Bible study once a month at the boys' detention center and will visit the County Jail once a month for Bible study. In addition, we will ask all church members to donate toiletries and socks for the inmates. We expect for this ministry to be a success and grow in the name of the Lord."

"If there is no other new business to discuss, I move this meeting be adjourned. We will meet again on the second Monday of next month. Good night, Deacons."

Michelle nervously moved around her Southside condominium, straightening and cleaning. She picked up the game disc cases Miller left all over the room from his various game consoles—Wii, X-Box, and Playstation—then moved on to pick up Miller's tennis shoes and jacket, strewn all over the room. *How can one child make such a mess all by himself?* Xavier was on his way, and she couldn't let him see the condo messy.

Michelle always cleaned when she was nervous. She was nervous because she had something very important to discuss with Xavier. She sent their seven-year-old son next door so they could have some privacy. It is Xavier's weekend to spend time with his son and for Miller to see the other side of his family. *He had better not leave my child over at his ex-wife's house. I don't know why she resents me and my child so much. Her marriage was over long before I started dating Xavier.*

Finally, her living space was as clean as it was going to get. Michelle attempted to relax as she walked into her spacious kitchen and headed straight to the cabinet next to the stove. The warm spring sun shined through her floor-to-ceiling windows just as it begun to set. Grabbing a wine glass, she filled it with sparkling grape juice as she admired her kitchen. It brought her so much peace and solace. She loved the lavender painted walls and stainless steel appliances. The exposed wooden beams throughout the condo exquisitely highlighted the condo's previous life as a warehouse. Her favorite room in the whole house was the great room with her specially-made eggplant leather sofa. She had it custom designed just for this space. She took her drink into the great room and sat on the sofa to get her thoughts together. *I could use something stronger to drink right now, but oh well . . .*

The doorbell chimed, interrupting her thoughts. Michelle reluctantly left her comfortable seat on the sofa and walked the short distance to the front door. Looking through the peephole, she saw Xavier standing there in his uniform with a lopsided grin on his face; that grin always made her grin too.

As she opened the large steel door, Xavier pushed past her heading straight for his favorite spot on the sofa. "So, what is this all about? Where is Miller?"

"Hello to you too, Xavier," Michelle said as she closed the door.

Xavier offered, "Hello," and stared intently at Michelle. She had always been a good-looking woman. That day she looked exceptionally nice in her tailored Donna Karen business suit and bare, manicured feet. She had a special glow about herself, too. "Sit down and let's get to business," Xavier said as he tried to shake off his naughty thoughts.

Michelle sat down next to him on the sofa as he stretched his long legs, took his gun out of its holster, and placed it on the end table. Before the gun touched the table, Xavier hesitated.

"Where is Miller, again?"

"I sent him next door to Ms. Jamison's so we can talk grown folk business."

"Oh really," Xavier's naughty thoughts returned.

Not that kind of business, Michelle thought, suddenly feeling uncomfortable. She stood to her feet, pacing and fidgeting. "Miller's grades are good, but he's been getting in trouble in class. "Will you have a talk with him, please?"

"Sure, I think I can handle that," Xavier answered.

"Thanks. Another thing, his class is taking a trip to the aquarium in Atlanta. Can you help me with the cost? I hate to ask you for additional money, but the housing market is not as good as it used to be and my commissions are slow coming in."

"You are killing the mood here," Xavier sighed. He pulled her back down on the sofa next to him. "I was hoping we could revisit the things we talked about a few months ago," he said with a hint of desire.

"Xavier, we've talked about this before," Michelle said firmly making eye contact. "That night was a mistake. We were both lonely and acted out of sheer emotion. We decided a relationship between us doesn't work. Keeping things physical will only confuse us and confuse Miller. Let's continue to raise our children as co-parents and accept that our romantic and physical relationship is over."

Looking puzzled due to her choice of words, Xavier asked, "We only have one child, Michelle. Do I have you stumbling over your words," Xavier said with a laugh. What is so important for us to discuss?"

Pacing once again, Michelle retorted, "Well, it is concerning that night."

About three months ago, Michelle was moping around her condo upset that a customer's financing, along with her commission, had fallen through at the last minute. To top it off, her current fling had cancelled their date for the third time in a row. She knew Derrick was no good for her, but he was good for a good time. It was also Xavier's weekend with Miller. Miller was over at Ms. Jamison's playing with her grandson, Parker, when Xavier had arrived a little earlier than usual. He smelled of the shower he took after a basketball game with his buddies on the force. He came in complaining about the argument he had with his ex-wife, Cheryl, right before his pick-up game. As Michelle tried to comfort and calm him down, emotions rose, compliments were whispered, and things got out of hand.

Michelle said soberly, "We didn't use protection that night."

"But you're on birth control, right?"

"Yeah. I was on birth control when I got pregnant with Miller too," she added, barely above a whisper.

"So what are you saying, Michelle?"

She responded calmly and looked Xavier square in the eyes, "I'm pregnant."

Xavier was stunned. He couldn't believe this was happening again because he couldn't take care of a fifth child. He was already struggling. Xavier reached into his pocket and pulled out his wallet.

Michelle gulped with tears forming, "Not this again."

Xavier jumped to his feet, "Michelle, you can't possibly think we can keep this baby. I already have four children. We do not have the resources to care for another child. You said so yourself, the housing market

47

is down." Xavier tried desperately to get Michelle to see things his way.

"I know this is hard to swallow. It's hard for me to accept as well. I've finally gotten into a routine caring for Miller, working and feeling confident I'm doing a great job of both. But Xavier, I've thought about it, and I just can't go through with an abortion."

"'Chelle, we have to think about this logically and not with our emotions. We have to think about our finances and resources. It will not be fair to Miller and to his brothers and sister." Michelle knew Xavier would not take this news well, but she did not expect him to insist on this course of action.

Trying to keep her anger in check, she responded in a low respectful tone, "It's supposed to be the woman's right to choose, right? This is my body and my child, and I must keep this child," she insisted. "We have to give this baby a chance at life. We had this conversation when we found out about Miller, and look what a joy he turned out to be."

"Well, if that's how you feel about it, I don't want any part of raising this child," Xavier declared throwing his hands up in exasperation. "You are doing this one on your own."

Michelle got in Xavier's face, "Please, do not make the hood in my mama come out of me. Babies come from sex. As long as you have sex with someone of the opposite gender, it will always be a possibility. If you don't want a baby, then don't have sex. If you have sex, you need to be prepared to live with the consequences. Man up, Xavier."

Xavier started pacing the space in front of the sofa trying to keep his composure. "This discussion is over." He flung the cash he had been holding in his hand in her face. "You take this money and have an abortion, or you make it stretch for 18 years. The choice is yours."

Michelle stepped up behind him as his pace slowed in front of the end table, grabbed his shoulder, and turned him around until he faced her. With one hand on her hip and one finger in his face, Michelle retorted, "If you insist, Xavier. I will go to family court when this child is born, we will take a DNA test, and set up child support payments to take the rest of your check. You can choose if this will be civilized or ruthless, but those are the only choices you have. I have decided to have this baby, and the State will make you care for it."

Xavier tried to push past Michelle, but she kept pulling him towards her.

Xavier picked up his gun from the end table and prepared to leave, "Move, Michelle. Tell Miller I'll catch him next time. I'm in no position to keep him now."

"Do not punish your child because you are mad at me!"

"I can't deal with this right now, Michelle, move out the way!" He shoved her slightly with his gun in his hand.

Michelle yelled, "I can't believe you put your hands on me," and shoved him back.

"Keep your voice down, 'Chelle, we don't want to get the whole building involved."

"The whole building needs to see how trifling a man you are."

"You got one more time to get in my face, 'Chelle." With the gun in his hand, Xavier tried to push past Michelle to get out of the door, but she wouldn't budge and started pounding on his chest. In a cloud of confusion, Xavier heard a loud sound and realized a bullet had discharged from the barrel of his gun. Michelle's petite five-feet-five frame crumbled to the floor in the entryway. In shock, Xavier stood in the partially opened door with his finger on the trigger.

~~~

The emergency waiting room at University Hospital was unusually quiet for a Friday night. No multiple cases of gunshot wounds or drunk-driving accident victims were present. Just Xavier and an elderly couple sat in the sterile, stark white room. Both of his hands balled up in fists over his mouth, Xavier's eyes were wide with a blank stare on his face. The day's events played on repeat in his mind like a Deep South gospel song with no joy. Just as he began to stand up to stretch his legs, Carol and Paul ran through the doors of the emergency room. Looking frantic in her light coat covering her shiny satin pink pajamas, Carol swiftly walked toward Xavier.

"What happened? Where's Miller? How is Michelle?"

Xavier stumbled over words trying to answer Carol's questions. When he realized what he had done, first he called an ambulance then Ms. Jamison to see if she would continue to watch Miller before calling the Roberts to tell them to meet him at the hospital.

Before he managed to get a word out, two Birmingham police officers approached them, one male and one female. "Officer Jordan," the male officer said, "my name is Officer Benton, and this is my partner Officer Jackson. We would like to have a few words with you in private down at the station. We understand you are a fellow officer; you serve and protect the students on this campus. We are sure this was just an accident, but we still have to take you in for questioning, you know how it goes."

Paul broke his silence, "I hate to break up this frat meeting, but what happened to my niece?" Paul directed his question to the officers then looked at Xavier. "What kind of accident was Michelle in?"

Carol cut her husband off, "Please, will someone please give us some details," she pled with tears running down her face.

"Ma'am," Officer Jackson said, "It seems there was a domestic dispute between your niece, Michelle Larsen, and her former boyfriend, Xavier Jordan. The neighbors reported loud talking coming from Ms. Larsen's condo. The loud talking escalated into yelling and a scuffle and resulted in a gunshot."

"Gunshot," Carol echoed as she sunk down in a chair with her eyes trained on Xavier.

Officer Jackson continued, "We need to take Officer Jordan into custody for questioning."

"Mrs. Roberts, Mr. Roberts," Xavier said begging with his eyes, "It was an accident, we were fighting, and I didn't intend to shoot her. It was an accident, I swear."

"Oh my God, Miller! Did Miller see this?" Carol said.

"No, he was next door playing with Parker. I didn't even see him tonight. He is still at Ms. Jamison's. I asked her to watch him."

Paul said, "I'll call Daniel and have him pick Miller up and take him to our house. He should be with family right now. So, what about Michelle? How is she doing?"

"We don't know yet. We are waiting for an update from the doctor. Officers, please do not take me now. I promise I will give you all the information you need but please let me see how Michelle is doing first."

"We can wait a little while, but we can't guarantee you for how long. We don't know how long an update will take," Officer Benton responded.

"Carol, are you going to be okay while I step outside to call Daniel?" Paul said.

"Go ahead, honey. Call Daniel and tell him what's going on."

As her husband walked out of the hospital door, Carol just sat and cried softly for Michelle. *Michelle is a strong young woman, Lord. She has worked hard and she can make it through this. Oh, Lord, she has to pull through. She has so much more life to live. She has little man to raise. What's going to happen to him? Oh, Lord.*

Paul came back in and sat next to her, rubbing her back. They all just sat there in silence while the police officers stood towering over them. After about fifteen minutes, Dr. Patel came in the waiting room. "Larsen family?"

"We are right here, Doctor," Carol and Paul said as they stood up.

"There was a lot of blood, and we couldn't stop the bleeding enough to save her. We did all we could. I'm so sorry to inform you we could not save the baby, but Ms. Larsen is still in critical condition. She could pull through; it's about a 50/50 chance."

"Baby, what do you mean 'baby?' What are you talking about losing a baby?"

"Michelle Larsen was approaching four months of pregnancy. We were unable to save the baby girl," Dr. Patel stoically reported.

Xavier got up from his seat to approach the Roberts. "That's what we were arguing about. She wanted to keep the baby and I didn't. We just can't afford another child."

"Mr. Jordan, you are under arrest for the attempted murder of Michelle Larsen," Office Benton announced as the old steel slammed against Xavier's thick wrists.

"Wait, wait, he would never intentionally hurt Michelle or his children. We believe him. It had to be an accident," Carol said.

"I'm sorry; we still have to take him into custody."

"I am so sorry, Mr. and Mrs. Roberts. It was an accident. Please understand. Let me know any updates on her condition." The officers walked out of the emergency room with Xavier in handcuffs.

~~~

Rev. Ashley made sure her Bluetooth was secure in her ear. Pulling out the Post-it note with Jodie's cell phone number written in Oneilia's bubbly script, she transcribed the digits to her cell phone before instructing it to call.

"J. Sutton," answered in her 'who is this calling my phone' voice.

"Hi, Jodie. This is Rev. Ashley. I'm glad I was able to reach you. I read your note soon after you gave it to me. It really pulled at my heart, and I'd like to talk more about it with you. Is right now a good time?"

"Umm . . . sure." Jodie didn't expect to hear from her so quickly. "You caught me off guard but, yeah, we can talk."

Rev. Ashley started, "I know it had to be difficult for you to reach out to me, but I'm glad you did. Something you may not know about me though is that I get straight to the point."

"Uh huh. . . "

"Tell me more about what is concerning you. When did you begin to feel like you were drowning?"

"You weren't exaggerating. You don't waste any time," Jodie said laughing nervously. "Umm . . . right after I graduated from college. I started doing things I thought I'd never do.

"What kind of things?"

"Things I know I shouldn't do," Jodie said as if talking to herself.

"You don't have to give me specific details but what areas do you feel you have messed up in?" Silence. I can sense your reluctance. Would you rather talk about this in my office or another time?"

"I'm okay. How can I put this? I have engaged in activities that show I didn't know my own worth. I didn't realize that at the time though. But now that I do, I still can't stop doing those wrong things."

Rev. Ashley silently prayed for the Holy Spirit to give her the right words to say because they were not getting anywhere on this path. "I have an idea. You expressed yourself so well in the note. If you don't feel comfortable talking about it, you can write down your feelings about the wrong decisions you think you've made. Your thoughts will be safe in God's hands."

"I do think I express myself much better in writing," Jodie said.

Rev. Ashley looked up to the heavens and mouthed, *thank you, Holy Spirit.* "Great, "she exclaimed for Jodie to hear.

"I agree I should write it down, but I would still like to share it with you. It's hard for me to say this, but I need your help. I've tried it many times on my own."

"I'm glad to help. None of us can make it on our own. I look forward to hearing from you. My email address is listed on my business card, please use it. I'll see you soon."

"Okay. I need to click over to see who this is blowing up my phone. Have a good night," Jodie ended the call.

Call waiting had been beeping nonstop throughout her conversation with Rev. Ashley. It was nobody but Amir, and she knew exactly what he wanted. When Rev. Ashley hung up, she noticed a text message from Pastor Longhorn. He asked her to meet him at University Hospital as soon as possible. Michelle

Larsen had been shot. Rev. Ashley immediately started to pray as she headed towards her car.

╫╫

Xavier sat in the interrogation room waiting for questioning. *How did I get here? How did things turn so ugly so quickly?* Xavier and Michelle's relationship had not always been so rocky. They had some very happy times during their friendship-turned-courtship.

When they met, it was a very difficult time in Xavier's life. Michelle was just the breath of fresh air he needed. He was going through a bitter divorce from his wife of 12 years. The mediator appointed by the court suggested they sell their family home and split the profits. The mediator knew the perfect real estate agent to sell their family home, Michelle Larsen.

Xavier couldn't keep his eyes off Michelle when he first met her. Not only was she beautiful, but also intelligent, confident, and financially independent! Michelle, knowing Xavier had just gotten out of a messy divorce, did not respond to his advances, yet their coincidental encounter at an African American young professionals mixer changed all that. Michelle was there networking, trying to expand her clientele. By chance, Xavier's friends from the force convinced him it was time to get out and meet new women. He couldn't believe his luck when his eyes landed on her.

Michelle stood with a group discussing the importance and benefits of home ownership. He waited patiently until she finished her conversation and managed to catch her eye in the process. She gave him a slight grin as she said her goodbyes to the group and began to walk in the opposite direction, but Xavier caught up to her before she could get away.

"Excuse me, Miss, may I have a moment of your time?"

She turned slightly toward him, "Every moment is precious. Why should I give you the   honor?"

I like a sassy woman. "How about you follow me to the bar on the Southside for drinks, and we can discuss it while sharing those precious moments over martinis?"

"Should you be socializing so soon after your divorce?" Michelle said while staring intently in his eyes trying to discern his true character.

He eventually convinced her to join him at Starbucks on the Southside a few days later. It wasn't the cocktail he wanted but coffee would suffice to get a chance to spend time with this captivating woman. They enjoyed themselves over coffee and developed a fast friendship.

About six months later, the nature of their relationship changed one night over dinner. It had been a long hard week, and Xavier was looking forward to a relaxing dinner with his good friend. He arrived at the restaurant before Michelle and sat at their usual table on the second level overlooking the bar area. He ordered her favorite drink and appetizer while waiting for her. Michelle arrived in a huff looking like she had run the ten blocks from her building. She was grateful he had a drink waiting on her. Michelle noticed in her hurried state that he was slumped over with weary eyes.

"So tell me, what's the matter?"

"What do you mean?" Xavier replied as he played with his drink.

"You look down."

"Really? You think you know me, huh?"

"Stop playing and tell me what's up."

"Me and the boys got haircuts today. I just dropped them off. I'm always down after I take the kids back to their mom."

"You and Cheryl get into it again?"

"Not exactly. While watching the kids go in the house, I couldn't help wondering how we ended up in separate homes. Cheryl and I did things the right way. We got married right after high school. We had been best friends since second grade.

"It has to be tough being reminded of your shattered dreams," Michelle said in a soft tone watching the band below set up for their nightly performance.

"Who you telling? Divorce was not supposed to be an option. We always planned for Cheryl to stay home with the kids when we started a family."

"Xavier, she just realized that wasn't enough for her. She wanted to work outside the home after the kids got older."

"Yeah, but her desire to go to school to become an interior designer strapped us financially and emotionally."

"You my boy and all, but I'm not going to let you put all the blame on her," Michelle added.

Xavier gave Michelle a menacing look. "All she had time for was schoolwork and the kids. Being the responsible man I am, I took on more work doing event security to bring in extra cash." Xavier seemed to be annoyed by the sound of the band warming up. He usually enjoyed their music but he wasn't exactly in a

59

jovial mood. And Michelle's observations didn't help, no matter how valid they were.

"You want a treat? That's what you are supposed to do."

"You know Michelle, one of the things I love about you is your quick wit, but can you slow your roll, please?

"Go 'head," Michelle said with a shrug.

"I wasn't used to going days without talking to my wife and many nights without touching her. When we did talk, it was all about the kids. In the end, we stopped talking at all. Now I only get to see my kids when it's convenient for Cheryl."

Michelle started talking louder as the band began, and the crowd got thicker on the first level. "I admire couples like my aunt and uncle. They have been together for I don't know how long, and they are still in love with each other. They said it's because they put God first in their relationship. Uncle Paul told me he loves and fears God too much not to honor his wife."

"I don't know if it's even possible to form relationships like theirs these days. Everybody is only out for themselves. Do you think you will ever have what your uncle and aunt have?" asked Xavier.

"I don't know. I don't spend much time worrying about it. I'm focused on my career right now," Michelle replied as she started grooving with the band.

With the tips of his fingers on her chin, Xavier turned her face back towards him, "Does your career keep you warm at night?"

She took hold of his hand, removed it from her face and gently placed it on his side of the table. "No, but the down duvet I bought with the money my career affords does."

"One point for Michelle!" Xavier said making an invisible tally mark in the air. "You have officially put me in my place."

As she laughed, Michelle asked, "What else is on your mind?"

"One of the guys on the force is having a birthday party for his wife next Saturday. Will you go with me?"

"Sure, I can be your stand in. What happened to Janelle? She can't find a babysitter?"

"She's available but I'd rather have you by my side, "Xavier said.

As Officer Benton and Officer Jackson entered the interrogation room, Xavier realized he was drenched in tears and sweat. He pulled his t-shirt up to his face as he used to do after schoolyard basketball games. Officer Jackson took a seat across from Xavier, meeting him at eye level and Officer Benton's John Henry-like stature hovered over the whole room. The compact space became smaller with all the big bodies now stuffed in it.

Officer Benton began the questioning, "What happened in that condo? How did Michelle Larsen end up shot, in the hospital fighting for her life and her unborn child dead? Explain that to us. Mr. Jordan, did you intentionally shoot Michelle Larsen?"

"No, I didn't shoot her on purpose. It was an accident," his eyes darted between the two officers and the dingy egg-white walls.

"Then why did you carry a loaded gun without the safety on into a household that included a small child, your child?" Officer Benton asked. "You are a trained officer, you know better than that. Do you think you are above the law, Mr. Jordan?"

"No, sir. I wish I could take back all the day's events. I certainly didn't mean to hurt Michelle. Yes, I was angry but I didn't mean to hurt her. I know it was a bonehead move, but I swear it was an accident. I give you my word, it was an accident," Xavier said as his voice cracked.

Officer Jackson responded, "Your word is of no value to us, Mr. Jordan." Her alarmingly soothing tone frightened him. "If that's the answer you are sticking with, let's go ahead and get your signed statement and proceed with booking you for attempted murder. If you believe in a god, you better call on him. . . or her. . . now."

~~~

Jodie sat in her living room staring at the vaulted ceiling, reflecting on her conversation with Rev. Ashley, while John Legend's *Once Again* album played from her iPod stereo. When the song, "Another Again," came on, she immediately set it to replay. By the third repeat, Amir had called five times and texted twice. She answered on the next ring so he would stop blowing up her phone. Bad decision. She caved in from a simple, "What's up?" Without much convincing, Jodie told Amir, "Be here in an hour. I'll leave the front door unlocked and wait for you upstairs."

As she prepared for his visit, she tried to shake the nagging feeling that she was just wasting her time, *"Why can't I let him go? I can't figure out why I'm so drawn to him. It is no way possible we could have any kind of future together."*

Amir arrived on schedule for a change with a red Kangol on his head, a red warm up suit on his body, and an energy drink in his hand. With few words spoken, Amir got undressed and joined Jodie in the king size bed.

They always enjoyed each other's company and as well as each other's bodies. On their last visit, they tried some new things that left bruises on Jodie's face and neck. It was fun, but she had a helluva time covering it up at church the next day, not to mention a truckload of guilt.

When they were done, Amir laid next to Jodie for a while taking in the moment; usually he got up right away to take a shower. Instead, he asked Jodie to bring him a towel, which she gladly did as he admired her every curve. As she handed it to him, he tugged on it causing her to fall on top of him. Giggling, Jodie rolled back over onto her side of the bed landing on her back. With both of them still holding on to the towel, Amir gave her a knowing look.

"Put a condom on," Jodie said.

With his dark skin pressed tightly against her body, Jodie started to feel a sharp pain in her abdomen. She ignored it, hoping it would quickly pass but it didn't. She had never experienced this kind of pain before. Maybe God was punishing her or warning her. Jodie cried out in distress, but Amir didn't seem to notice because his moves became rougher resulting in more pain.

Noticing the tension in her body Amir said "I can't tell if your cries are of pleasure or of pain." He didn't wait for any clarification though.

Unable to bear it any longer, she mustered up enough sweetness to whisper, "I'm ready if you are," which he knew was code for finish up because I'm done. It's rude to blatantly say stop when you've already consented. But Amir ignored her request and intentionally delayed his orgasm.

Jodie shrieked, "Stop," and tried to pull away.

With a strong grip, Amir growled, "I'm not finished yet."

Jodie stiffened not knowing what to do. She knew he wouldn't be happy about her request, but she didn't expect him to be cruel. He could easily overtake her and get away with it. None of Jodie's family or friends had ever even heard of him. *What has gotten into him? What can I do? It's like I'm not even in the room.* The tears fell heavier, and she began to wail. Eventually he crawled off her without climaxing; they laid there in silence for what seemed like hours.

Amir broke the silence, "Are you asleep?"

She looked at him sideways, "No."

"Since your stuff is tender, can I get some head?" Jodie laid there in disbelief waiting for him to catch the hint that playtime was over, and he should go. *He probably doesn't think anything went wrong. Do I even understand what just happened?*

Finally, he got up, made a pit stop in the bathroom, and then left the house without saying a word.

~~~

Daniel couldn't get Miller to go to sleep. He had not told him anything about what happened to his mother, but he was sure Miller noticed the bad vibes. Daniel tried to keep him busy playing the Wii. Miller was beating Daniel at tennis when his cell phone rang. As he put the game on pause, Miller complained, "Aw, man, I was just about to beat you for the third time in a row."

"Hold on, little man. Hello,"

"Hey Danny, any word yet?" Wynsome asked. They had gotten really close during the seven months they had been together.

"No changes to report. She is still in critical condition," Daniel said in a hushed tone making sure not to say his cousin's name.

"Do you want me to keep you company while you wait?"

"No, it's late. You shouldn't be out on the road this time of night."

"I'm coming over anyway. You should not be alone, Daniel. I know she is like a sister to you and you are worried and you are trying to keep it cool for Miller's sake."

"You're right, but I can handle it. I'll see you tomorrow."

"I'm on my way, Danny. I'll be there in 15."

"Danny, can we get back to our game now," Miller squealed.

"Yeah, little man."

"I'll see you when you get here, Wyni," Danny said. "I love you."

"I love you, too."

"Wyni is coming over too! Now I can beat both of y'all behinds," Miller said.

You know your aunt Carol would whip your behind for saying behind," Daniel said as they got back to playing Wii tennis.

When Wynsome arrived, Daniel was trying to get his seven-year-old second cousin to go to bed. By 10:30, Daniel still hadn't received an update from his parents. He really hadn't had an opportunity to process the whole situation. *How did Xavier accidentally shoot Michelle?* He struggled to focus on something else to keep from worrying himself sick.

Wynsome loved spending time with Daniel's family. She couldn't wait until she was officially a part of it. Daniel had mentioned marriage a few times, but they haven't talked about it at length. In the beginning, Wynsome tried really hard not to fall for the church boy, but he won her over.

While Miller put up the video game, Daniel loaded the dishwasher. It hurt Wynsome's heart to see the troubled look on Daniel's face. She stepped up to the opposite side of the opened dishwasher door, leaned over and gave him a passionate kiss. Their lips lingered together a little longer than necessary. Daniel closed the door and pulled Wynsome into a tight embrace.

Remembering what they were there to do, Wynsome and Daniel tag-teamed to get Miller bathed and in the bed. After he was in his Spiderman pajamas, Wynsome and Daniel followed Miller to his room; the same room Michelle had slept in when she lived there. They crawled into the bed with him and read him a bedtime story. When they were finished, Wynsome asked about the latest news at school.

Miller began, "Today in class, Parker drew something that looked like a soda can. He thinks he's going to be an artist. When Mrs. Jones asked what he was drawing, he said it was a can of Miller Lite, and the whole class laughed. Then I said, 'at least I wasn't conceived in a high school!' Wynsome sat straight up with her mouth agape.

"Miller, how do you know the word conceived? Do you even know what it means?"

"It's where babies come from, and Parker came from Parker High School. I hear Ms. Jamison tell him that all the time."

"Oh, okay," Wynsome said with a laugh but stopped short when she heard the house phone ringing.

"Hello. . .," Daniel answered.

"Daniel, is Miller asleep yet?" Paul asked.

"No, sir. Is everything alright?"

"You all should get to the hospital as soon as possible," Paul insisted.

When Daniel, Wynsome, and Miller arrived at the hospital, it was teeming with activity. Nurses and nurses' aides were swarming all over the place as Daniel frantically looked for Paul and Carol. As he approached the nurses' station to get information about Michelle, a code he didn't understand was called over the intercom system. Seemingly, all the hospital employees hurriedly disappeared behind a curtain. Daniel was then able to spot his father casually walking with a cup of coffee in his hand with Rev. Ashley at his side.

Rushing to Paul, Daniel asked, "Dad, what's going on? How is Michelle?"

"Daniel! You finally got here. I'm so happy to see you. Michelle has been asking for you. She wants to see you and Miller as soon as possible." Paul handed Daniel his cup of coffee so he could pick up Miller. Miller was too big to carry, but Paul just wanted to be close to him.

"Hey, Uncle Paw Paul," Miller said sleepily. "Is my mom sick?"

"Yes she is, little man, but she is in the hospital so they can help her get better."

Paul turned to greet Wynsome, "How are you, Wyni? I'm sorry Daniel has you out so late."

"Mr. Roberts, if I weren't here, I would be at home worrying anyway."

Smiling at Wynsome, "Is 'Chelle going to be okay?" Daniel said turning his attention back to his dad.

"She's doing great. The surgery went well. They were able to remove most of the b-u-l-l-e-t and stop the bleeding. They are preparing to take her to a room now. I'm sorry about the frantic phone call, but we were so excited when she woke up. As soon as she was able to speak, she asked to see you and Miller. You can go in as soon as they get her settled in the critical care unit."

"When will that be?"

"It shouldn't be much longer," Paul said.

"Where's Mom?"

"She was filled with a lot of nervous energy and couldn't be still so I suggested she go to Michelle's condo and bring back her necessities."

"Oh yeah, we brought mom an overnight bag." Daniel said. "It was Wyni's idea."

"Great! She will greatly appreciate that. Your mom went to Michelle's condo with an escort because it is still being examined by the p-o-l-i-c-e. She should be back before long. Pastor Longhorn and Rev. Ashley came by to pray with us. Pastor had to leave to visit another church member in another hospital," Paul said remembering Rev. Ashley was there.

"It's good to see you, Daniel, and Wynsome, but not under these circumstances," Rev. Ashley said giving them both a hug and rubbing Miller's back. It looks like you all are holding up well. I will continue to pray."

"Paw Paul, why are you spelling out your words? Is your school having a spelling bee too? Police was one of my spelling words but not bullet. Don't bullets go in the guns policemen like my daddy carry to protect people?" Miller asked.

As Uncle Paul struggled to find an answer, a nurse walked up, "Larsen family?" Paul breathed a sigh of relief for the distraction.

"That would be us," Daniel said.

"Ms. Larsen is settled in the critical care unit. You may go see her but only for a short while," the nurse informed them.

Rev. Ashley accompanied the family through the long, confusing corridors of University Hospital as they searched for Room 15A in the critical care unit.

Daniel spotted the room first and peeked inside to see a pasty-looking Michelle sleeping. Only the light over her head was on; casting shadows on the other walls. It was scary for Daniel to see Michelle hooked up to all those tubes, wires, and machines. Michelle was a strong young woman, but she looked so fragile at this moment. Everyone stood nervously at the door not wanting to be the first to go in. Carol approached from behind, catching everyone off guard.

"Hey, why is everyone standing out here? What's wrong?" Carol asked.

"We are afraid of what we may find in there," Daniel responded for all of them.

"Look, the Lord has given us His love and power to overcome the spirit of fear. Do not forget who is really in charge here." Shifting Michelle's lavender overnight bag from one hand to the other, Carol continued "Now, Daniel and Paul, you go. She won't bite, I'm sure. Not today anyway."

Reluctantly, they went in while Carol and Wynsome stayed behind. Miller had fallen asleep in Paul's arms and had begun to put a strain on his back. Paul laid him down in the chair next to the hospital bed to get some relief. Paul stood to the left side of the bed while Daniel stood close to her head with Rev. Ashley on the right side. Michelle began to stir under their heavy stares. When she opened her eyes, she saw troubled faces looking down at her.

"Why is everyone hovering over me?" Michelle said in a weak voice. "Is there something I need to know?"

"We all wanted to be the first to see you wake up. We're sorry if we alarmed you," Rev. Ashley said with a smile, taking Daniel's place to get closer to Michelle. "I am so happy to see your bright eyes open. I'd like to pray for you and then I'll leave so your family can visit with you privately." Rev. Ashley took hold of Michelle's hand and began to pray softly but passionately and authoritatively. Her touch startled and soothed Michelle at the same time. Rev. Ashley's touch felt like God was touching her directly.

After she finished praying, Rev. Ashley said her goodbyes. Paul asked Daniel to step out as well while he talked to Michelle alone. He waited until Daniel was completely out before saying anything, relieved Miller was still asleep.

"Do you remember what happened tonight?"

"All I remember is...is that my little man over there? Aww, he looks so cute and harmless when he's asleep. That's mommy's baby . . . baby. . .," a look of sorrow overtook Michelle's face. "My baby," she whispered.

She discovered a large, bloody bandage when she placed her hand on her stomach. Suddenly aware of the pain, she pushed the button on the Morphine pain pump.

"Me and Xavier got into . . . an argument." Michelle dozed off after every few words but woke up starting exactly where she left off. "Where is that son of a bi. . . .?" Remembering who she was talking to, Michelle changed her tone and choice of words, "The argument got pretty heated, then I remember pain, excruciating pain, then I blacked out. Uncle Paul, what happened to my. . ."

"Baby?" Uncle Paul said finishing her sentence. "Xavier's gun accidentally discharged, and he shot you in the abdomen. I'm sorry, but you lost the baby. They couldn't save her. Thankfully, your surgery went well, and you are still with us. They were able to retrieve the bullet. You lost a lot of blood, but you made it through, 'Chelle. Praise the Lord!"

So, it was a girl? I lost my baby, my baby girl?" Michelle broke down in sobs. Paul sat on the bed and tried to hold her, causing Michelle to wince from the sharp pain in her stomach. She pressed the Morphine pump again.

"I'm sorry, 'Chelle. I don't know why these things happen."

"And Xavier?" Michelle said with a look of disgust on her face.

"They took him in for questioning. Rest assured, God does love you and he will take good care of you through this whole ordeal. I'm going to let the rest of the family come in, and I will step out for a moment. Is that okay?"

"Yeah, Unc, that's fine," Michelle said, staring at nothing or no one in particular.

Paul walked into the hallway to find Daniel, Wynsome, and Carol still talking to Rev. Ashley. After giving everyone the okay to go in, Paul began to walk down the hallway.

Carol called after him, "Paul, you're not coming in with us?"

"No, I'm going to take a walk. Keep a close eye on her."

"Baby, she will be alright. She's in the Lord's hands."

"I know, I know," Paul said quickening his pace.

Rev. Ashley said to Wynsome, "Would you like to reschedule our meeting for tomorrow due to the circumstances?"

Wynsome hesitated giving Daniel a questioning look. When he nodded his head in the affirmative, Wynsome told Rev. Ashley they could keep their appointment.

~~~

Paul meandered down the hallway and made a left turn, ending up in front of the service elevator. The feeling of his cell phone vibrating caught him off guard. He smiled when he saw the caller I.D. reporting Oneilia Sutton calling. Oneilia always had an encouraging word, and that's exactly what he needed right now.

Before Paul could completely say, "Hello," Oneilia was already talking. "Deacon Paul Roberts, I heard what happened to your baby girl. I know Carol didn't give birth to her, but y'all raised her just as your own. Now you know the Lord is close to the brokenhearted. This situation has to have your heart broken but remember, our God has the last word, not no doctor, not no nurse, and not no odds. He ain't no gambling man, either, so don't listen to what they say about survival rates and what not. I just wanted to encourage you and let you know I'm praying."

Oneilia hung up before Paul even had a chance to say thank you. That's Oneilia; she leaves no room for back talk.

~~~

Wynsome pulled into the parking lot at the church. The huge structure was eerie without all the people who filled it on Sunday mornings. Her stiletto booties tapped loudly on the wooden corridors as she looked for the door labeled Youth Director. Just when Wynsome spotted the door, Rev. Ashley opened it before Wynsome even had a chance to knock. Quickly, Rev. Ashley ushered her in, mouthed a soft welcome, and offered Wynsome a seat. In a fast pace, Rev. Ashley walked back to her desk and sat Indian style in her plush brown leather chair. Rev. Ashley had a comfortable, simple style. She had on a slightly wrinkled button-down white shirt, jeans, crocs, and no makeup. Her hair was in the usual messy ponytail. Rev. Ashley is what some fashion editors call an accidental beauty.

"I'm so glad to see you. I wasn't sure if you would be up to it considering this trying time. I know the Roberts must be really stressed out right now. I am confident Michelle will come through victoriously, though," Rev. Ashley began.

"Really? How can you be so sure?"

"Honestly, whatever the outcome, it will be victorious because the One who has already overcome the world is in control. That's what I have to keep reminding myself."

"I don't know what any of that means," Wynsome said dismissively, a little tired of all the super spiritual talk she had been hearing lately. "I still wanted to come by because I needed someone to talk to about all of this. I am so worried. I care a lot about Daniel, and I know Daniel cares a lot about his family. I don't know how to act. What does a good girlfriend do in a situation like this? I'm not good with all that emotional stuff. I'm not sure if I'm being of much help to him right now," Wynsome responded, taking off her jacket and placing her feet on the matching ottoman in front of her.

"I'm sure he appreciates you just being there. It doesn't take a lot of words or grand gestures. Our loved ones are grateful for our presence and the sacrifice of our time."

"Thank you. I needed to hear that."

"So, you are probably wondering why I wanted to meet with you."

"I am a bit curious," Wynsome answered honestly.

"I'm glad you agreed to come. I want to get to know all the attendants of Truthseekers personally. I have heard great things about your musical talents, and I've seen your wonderful planning and organizing skills."

"Music is my passion," Wynsome said perking up.

"Would you like to share your passion in some way at the church?" Rev. Ashley asked, matching her enthusiasm.

"I am flattered that you ask, but you do know I'm not a member of this church. I'm not a member of any church, and I'm not looking for a church, either."

"Yes, I am aware, but you have visited quite frequently with Daniel, and you are already a member of Truthseekers." Rev. Ashley got up and went to the mini fridge in the corner of her office. She took out a bottle of water and a Buffalo Rock, holding them up for Wynsome to choose. Wynsome took the water. Everyone always chooses the water.

"Rev. Ashley, Daniel and I support each other in everything. He is really into this church stuff, so I come to spend time with him. He knows I'm not big on it and doesn't force it on me either. That's one of the things I love about him. In turn, he attends the symphony and Broadway plays with me."

"I have seen the two of you together and I can see the mutual admiration. You two seem to have a great relationship. We need more young people like you to be involved at the church. Since you will be here, you might as well get involved."

"I suppose. I am just not the 'church' type. I don't think like these people."

"These people need to start thinking differently," Rev. Ashley said. "It will benefit us to have un-indoctrinated people like you offering their insight so we can reach more young people. Our church needs some radical change," Rev. Ashley added.

"It already seems pretty radical to me. I didn't know Miami bass was allowed in the church."

"It has advanced in some ways but the true spirit of the church leadership has not changed. Let me give you a little church history lesson. When my daddy started bringing me here in 1983, we held services in an old boys and girls club with about fifty members. After I moved away, Rev. Longhorn became the pastor, and the church grew quickly in attendance and stature. Even though we have become a larger, Holy Spirit-filled place of worship, those same fifty people who started in that boys and girls club are still here, trying to take back control of 'their church,' my dad, Ruben Rouser, being one of them."

"Yeah, I've heard of him," Wynsome responded.

"Girl, everybody has and not in a good way. Even though he's my daddy, that dead, traditional spirit in him and the other 49 needs to go, in Jesus name!"

~~~

The next morning a nurse woke Michelle to check her vital signs then cleaned her wound and changed her bandages. Dr. Patel walked in with her team of fresh-faced interns doing their morning rounds, interrupting Nurse Collins performing her duties.

"How is my patient doing this morning?" Dr. Patel asked.

"I'm doing fine, except for this excruciating pain in my stomach."

Michelle's skin had not returned to its normal caramel color, and she could barely keep her eyes open. The slightest move caused the utmost pain. She couldn't wait until she was back in her own bed.

"Well, that's to be expected. Your surgery went great, and you are doing very well. If you keep this up, you should be able to go home by Tuesday morning. If you don't have any questions for me, we will give you a quick once over and be on our way so you can rest."

Searching her foggy brain, Michelle finally responded, "I don't believe I have any questions."

"You do understand about the baby?" Dr. Patel asked looking directly into Michelle's eyes, giving her her full attention.

"Yes, I am aware."

"I am sorry for your loss. Don't worry, you should be able to conceive again," Dr. Patel said as she briefly gripped Michelle's forearm then returned to her examination. "Your blood pressure is a bit low. We will keep an eye on that. We expect it to improve soon. We are doing everything in our power to keep you comfortable."

"Thank you, Dr. Patel." The doctor told the nurse to move Michelle to a private room as soon as one became available. To Michelle's surprise, a male nurse moved her into a private room within the hour.

When Michelle settled in her room, Carol was permitted to stay with Michelle as long as she liked instead of the short time visitors were allowed to stay in the cold, stark intensive care waiting room she had slept in the night before.

"How are you really feeling?" Carol inquired.

"I have severe pain in my stomach, and I think the medication is making me nauseous but other than that, I can't complain. Did you sleep well in the waiting room chair last night?" Michelle asked her aunt, trying to divert the attention from her.

"My back is a little sore but I can't complain either," Carol said with a wide smile on her face. "I'm so happy you are sitting up."

"Auntie, I'd really like to see Daniel and Miller this morning," Michelle stressed.

"Why, 'Chelle? You asked for them last night. Remember? They came to see you."

"Yeah, I remember, but I was so heavily medicated, I couldn't stay awake long enough to talk to them. Can you make sure I see them today?"

"I will give Daniel a call after I come from the bathroom."

While Carol was freshening up, someone knocked on the hospital room door. Michelle strained to yell *come in* loud enough for them to hear. To her surprise, it was Daniel and Miller. Quickly, Miller spotted his mom, and his little feet aimed directly for the hospital bed. When he was a half inch away from his mark, he flipped over the rail and landed next to her in the bed.

"Hey, Mommy," he said huffing and puffing.

Whimpering, Michelle answered, "Hey, little man; be careful. Mommy's sore."

"Sorry, Mommy," Miller said as he snuggled close to her as she playfully smacked his bottom and planted kisses all over his face.

"Did Daniel and Uncle Paw Paul take good care of you last night?"

"Yeah, I beat Danny at baseball on the Wii and Uncle Paw Paul made blueberry pancakes this morning. You never make pancakes."

Michelle chuckled then clutched her stomach, "Would you like to watch TV with Mommy?"

"Yes, ma'am."

Carol emerged from the restroom looking refreshed and gave both Daniel and Miller a peck on the cheek. "I was just about to call you, Daniel. 'Chelle has been asking for you."

"Oh yeah? "Daniel said looking at Michelle with confusion.

Daniel encouraged his mother to go home and rest while he and Miller stayed with Michelle. Surprisingly, Carol agreed with no hesitation. She made him promise to take good care of Miller and Michelle before gathering her belongings and leaving.

Daniel settled into the deceptively comfortable chair next to the hospital bed. The cartoon channel had completely captivated Miller's attention, and Michelle was dozing on and off. Flower deliveries and phone calls from concerned family and friends came in constantly. Daniel discouraged any visitors so Michelle could rest and build up her strength.

Michelle woke up just as the lunch cart rolled in. Daniel helped her arrange the bedside tray in a comfortable position. They reminisced, laughed, and teased each other while she ate and Miller took a nap. During a break in her conversation with Daniel, Michelle glanced over at a sleeping Miller and suddenly developed a somber look on her face.

"Daniel, why did God kill my baby?"

"Wow, I didn't see that coming. Umm. . .God didn't kill your baby," Daniel answered self-assuredly.

"I know Xavier was the one who shot me, but God could have prevented any of this from happening, right? Why didn't He stop it? You and your parents are always talking about how God is in control."

"I still believe God is in control, and I know God loves you. We may never know why you lost your little girl, but ask Him to show you the purpose for your pain."

"Don't start with all that Bible-thumping talk now, Danny. I am not in the mood. I want to be so angry with God right now," Michelle said, clenching her teeth.

"I know, and it's okay to confess those thoughts and feelings to God. I can imagine this is very difficult for you, and you are tempted to focus only on the child you lost, but try to think about all you still have. The Lord spared your life, He protected Miller from seeing what happened, and you have loving family members and friends who are praying for you."

"I've thought about those things too, Daniel. I am so thankful God spared my life. When I got pregnant with Miller, I thought my life would go completely downhill from there, but your parents' support and love helped me keep pushing to reach my goals despite being a single mom. Not everyone has that kind of support. God has been with me this whole time and I'm thankful, but why didn't He save my little girl, too, Daniel? Why did my little girl have to die?"

"I don't have the answer to that question, 'Chelle, but we could ask the person who does. Pray with me?" Daniel asked holding his hands out palms up.

"Umm, I guess so but my little girl is still going to be dead. Praying won't change that."

"Let's just try Him."

Resigning, Michelle bowed her head. . .

"Dear Lord, we humbly come to you today, thanking you for sparing Michelle's life. Thank you for the healing taking place in her body and soul right now. Lord, we know you love us and that your love will never end. We know you will not stop working in us until your will is perfected in us. Increase our desire for only your will to be done in our lives. Help Michelle see you operating in her circumstances. Lord, she is angry right now because of the loss of her daughter. Please help her to forgive Xavier and to have peace throughout this ordeal; peace that transcends all understanding. We know it will take time, Lord. Help us to trust more in you every day. Help us to keep the faith you are working all things out for our good. . ."

A waterfall of tears fell down Michelle's face as Daniel continued to pray.

"Michelle, I believe the Lord is moving in your heart right now. Do you feel that, too?"

"Yes," Michelle sobbed.

"Do you feel God's desire for you to accept Christ's redemption today?" Daniel asked staring into Michelle's eyes.

She held up her tear-stained face, "Yes."

"Okay, pray this prayer with me. Lord, I ask you to come into my heart today. I believe your son Jesus Christ died on the cross for my sins. I confess all of my sins to you and ask for your forgiveness. I accept your son Jesus as my Lord and Savior on this day. From this day forward, I will walk in my God-given position as an over-comer and a saint. In Jesus' name, I pray. Amen."

Daniel held Michelle tightly as she cried tears of joy. Miller was wide awake now and gawking at them.

"Why is Mommy crying?"

"She is happy she just decided to serve Jesus!"

"Oh," Miller said, leaned over, gave his mother a kiss, and turned the TV up to watch more cartoons. Daniel and Michelle both laughed.

$$\cancel{||||} \ ||$$

To: Rev.J.Ashley@church.org
From: J_Sutton@southerntraditionsmail.com
Subject: Per our conversation

Rev. Ashley,

I've been thinking about your suggestion to write my feelings down. I actually do journal but not on a regular basis. I was going through some of my old journals and came across a poem I wrote not too long ago. Tell me what you think. . .

Go For What You Know
I knew
the first time I laid eyes on him he was not the one.
When I saw him walk into that classroom,
I thought
he is very attractive.
The first time he sat next to me his intoxicating smell overtook me
The first time I heard him speak
I heard resolve, drive, and ingenuity behind those words

And
Our first conversation
He granted me admission behind the music

I thought
I knew
He was not the one

Yet, I was attracted to or otherwise distracted by
his tall, dark frame and smooth black skin
I was moved by his dreams and aspirations
He was about to make things happen

Despite the constant knows going on in my head
The knows were quieted by the possibilities
The potential
I'm grown and I'm free-with no accountability
I've held out for how long? There's nothing wrong
with a little indulgence
Is there?
What am I depriving myself for?

At that point
I abandoned all the things I'd learned about God
My emotions acted in isolation of the Spirit of God's
Word
The mark that cannot be erased became blurred
This created the optimum environment for the
occurrence of my first time,
my first time
ever
That I can never ever get back

All the advice I'd given to friends suddenly flooded my
brain
Don't you have self-control?

Don't you know that God has other plans for that?
Now I'm faced with answering those same questions
For myself
And I realize that I was only speaking from head
knowledge.

The head knowledge acknowledges that there is
consequence for sin
I decided to act independently of God and give my
body in total worship
And
Tying my soul with another human being
God's will discounted, and purity vanished

If I continue to willfully do what I know to be wrong
I also must acknowledge that the wages of sin is death
God can and God will
take His grace and protection away
from me
I know too much about who God is to stay where I am
now.
I don't want new birth in the form of a fatherless
infant
And I don't want death
So,
I must
get up, dust myself off, and get back in line
and abide by the covenant that my God designed for
me

Taking heed from the Secular Prophet Green
To know who you are is to know who you are not

And

when you know who you are then you know who
everybody else is
Beloved, go for what you know
Beloved, go for what you know
Beloved, go for what you know

J. Sutton

~~~

Wynsome's birthday had arrived, and Daniel had been putting together her surprise for months now. He never imagined a tragedy like this would happen to his family and especially not in the midst of planning her celebration. Fortunately, he didn't have to forfeit his plans. Soon after Daniel's parents arrived, Mrs. Jamison and Parker came to pick up Miller for the night. Even though they fuss and fight, Parker and Miller had been friends since birth. Michelle and Parker's mother were good friends growing up despite their four year age difference. They became moms around the same time. Parker's mom, fortunately, had married a wealthy, older doctor and moved to Atlanta rather quickly after they met. Parker stayed with his grandmother most of the year. Mrs. Jamison didn't want him snatched from his home simply because of his mother's fly-by-night tendencies. Parker's stepdad leased Mrs. Jamison's condo for her.

"Mrs. Jamison, thank you so much for keeping Miller tonight," Michelle said.

"It's the least I could do, honey, judging by the condition you're in. I've always thought you were a good mother. Too bad you lost that baby. Did they tell you if you could have more babies?" Michelle kept smiling even though Mrs. Jamison's questions were getting too personal.

"I better go. I can't be late for my date with Wynsome," Daniel said, trying to change the subject.

"You and that girl still dating? I think she is a little too fast for you, if you ask me. Where her and her folks go to church?" Mrs. Jamison said, rolling right along with the change in subject. She had an opinion about everything!

"They don't have an official church home. Wynsome has been attending church with us since we've met though." Ms. Jamison has a membership at the historic 16th Street Baptist Church but hadn't stepped a foot in it since 1979. She still sent her tithe by her niece every month, though.

"You don't say. I still think she's fast. I would keep my eye on her if I were you, Carol. You've been keeping your thing in your pants?" Mrs. Jamison said, not missing a beat.

Paul jumped in, "Now, Hazel, do you think that is appropriate conversation with these boys in the room?"

"I was just saying. . ."

"Say no more," Paul said definitively.

"Okay fam, I'm out!" Daniel said, quickly leaving the room with his face flushed with embarrassment.

~~~

Daniel went to campus after leaving the hospital. He hadn't been there much because he had been staying at his parent's house helping his dad with Miller.

When Daniel entered his room, Brian sat on his bed folding laundry. He is the most meticulous guy Daniel has ever met. "Hey buddy, I haven't seen you for a few days. What's going on?" Brian asked.

"Oh, I have a little family situation going on, but everything will work out okay."

"I'm sorry to hear that, is it your parents?"

"Nah, my cousin Michelle is in the hospital, but she will be fine. Just keep us in your prayers."

"There is a traditional Baha'i prayer of healing for women. It basically asks for protection from every ailment and evil that may try to overtake her. Everyone can relate to that."

"Of course, but God is the only one who can get that done," Daniel replied as he laid his body on his twin bed. He felt all the tension from the last few days escape from his limbs.

Brian added, "Right. In the Baha'i faith, we also believe that there is only one God."

"Oh okay, cool. So you believe in Jesus, too? Daniel asked excitedly.

"Yeah, but not necessarily as the Messiah. We believe that two prophets have come after him as messengers of God."

"And now we discover the difference between the two religions. Thanks Brian for sharing that with me. I have always been fascinated by other religions. And thank you for keeping my cousin in your thoughts and prayers. Tonight, we cut loose and have big fun. Are you ready to party tonight for my girl's birthday? I have something really special planned."

"Special? Are y'all going to finally hook up?"

"I told you, we are waiting until we get married. The whole evening will be full of surprises for her, though. After drinks with y'all, we will head downtown for dinner at an expensive restaurant in a nice hotel, 'just the two of us'," Daniel said singing. He sat up to remove his shoes and socks, preparing to take a shower.

"You are taking her to a hotel? You sure you're not planning to hit that?"

"Is that all you think about, Brian? There's more to a relationship than the physical. I love this girl, and I'm not trying to do anything to mess this relationship up."

"Then you need to have sex with her. I know you're a virgin, but is she?"

"No, what are you trying to say?"

"I just said it. Maybe you are committed to waiting until marriage, but I don't think she is. She wouldn't mind getting down at all," Brian added.

"Nobody said it's been easy for us not to. But we both are committed to doing things God's way."

"I hate to break it to you like this, but the commitment is more on your end."

Daniel hurriedly grabbed his toiletry bag. "I can promise you nothing is going to happen."

In the bathroom, Daniel quickly took a shower, shaved, and went back into the bedroom to get dressed. He could faintly hear Brian and their other suitemates' animated voices in the common area. Brian, Ernest, and

Burke's voices faded after Daniel heard the loud thud of the suite's front door.

Good. They are finally gone. I was afraid they would be late. I don't know why I gave them the responsibility of securing our table at the restaurant.

Daniel began to think hard about Brian's comments about his relationship with Wynsome. *Maybe I am more dedicated to this celibacy thing than Wynsome is. She has made it clear she is willing if I am willing. I'll have to ask her about that, but not tonight.*

Daniel's phone vibrated at the same time he picked it up to call Wynsome. He looked down at the caller I.D. and saw she beat him to it. "Hey, Wyni."

Daniel could feel Wynsome's smile through the phone. "Hey, Danny, what time should I expect you?"

"I was just about to call you. Are you ready? I can head towards your dorm now."

"Yeah, I'm ready for my surprise. I have a surprise for you, too."

"It's supposed to be all about you tonight."

"I want to show you how special you are to me."

"I can't wait for this," Daniel grinned into the phone. "I'm on my way."

When Daniel pulled up in front of Wynsome's dorm, she was standing in front waiting for him. Daniel opened the door for her, admiring her formfitting, black cocktail dress with the back out. All of her best assets were on display. Her long hair was pulled up, showing her long neck and accentuating her striking cheekbones. Her pretty feet were clad in five-inch, strappy sandals highlighting her toned thighs and calf muscles. All those years of gymnastics had definitely paid off on her figure.

Daniel had never seen her dressed so sexy. When she approached him, she whispered 'surprise' in his ear.

"This is my surprise?" Daniel said with his mouth half open.

"Yes, I bought this dress with you in mind," Wynsome told him with a seductive smile.

"I am surprised." Daniel replied. He couldn't keep his eyes off her.

Wynsome was pleased that she had achieved her goal. She had been preparing for this night for weeks now. She searched both in Birmingham and Atlanta for the perfect outfit. She finally found it in a boutique in Atlanta's Little Five Points. It had been waiting there just for her; she was convinced of it.

Wynsome asked, "So what are our plans for the evening?" It was hard for Wynsome to allow Daniel to plan the whole celebration. She was afraid that he wouldn't get it right and she wouldn't have a good time.

"It is a surprise. I thought about blindfolding you but I knew you would just find a way to cheat anyway." Daniel drove out the front gate of Agee- Gadsden University and turned left, heading for the expressway. Soon the couple pulled into a parking space in front of the restaurant.

"Oh, I've heard about this place. They are supposed to have great sushi. But you hate sushi, Daniel."

"But you love sushi, Wyni."

Wynsome leaned over and gave Daniel a peck on the cheek before he guided her out of the car. They held hands as they walked up the steps and onto the patio of the restaurant. Ernest, Brian, Jodie, and Emberli were there waiting for them. Burke had an upperclassman who happened to be in the school's orchestra with Wynsome on his arm. Jodie and Emberli didn't know Wynsome very well; they were only familiar with her from Truthseekers. Daniel asked them to come because Wynsome didn't have any female friends.

Due to the wind, they opted to sit in the inside lobby instead of the outdoor patio as they originally planned. The lobby was narrow and tight. They were lucky to snag the conversation pit in the far right hand corner of the lobby.

When their orders arrived, Burke offered Daniel a taste of his salmon skin roll.

"Here, Daniel, taste this," Burke said as he tried to feed it to Daniel. Daniel quickly turned his head and Burke smashed the roll on the side of Daniel's face, missing his original target.

Chuckling, Brian said, "Eat the cake, Anna Mae."

As Daniel wiped the sticky rice off his face, everyone roared in laughter at Brian's *What's Love Gotta Do With It* reference; everyone except for Wynsome. Daniel was even amused and took it all in stride.

Looking annoyed, she said, "Oh, so you Ike Turner now? What does an Asian boy know about Ike and Tina? Y'all play too much. You need to grow up, Brian. You too, Burke. Wynsome has told Daniel countless times he needed to stop hanging out with these immature little boys.

After Wynsome calmed down with a cocktail in her hand, they talked and laughed, shared sushi, and sipped on fruity cocktails—everyone except Daniel. Daniel hated sushi and tried not to drink, but he knew

Wynsome craved this type of atmosphere. She was such a fun-loving and outgoing girl. They balanced each other out because Daniel was more laid back. This was her night and they were going to do things she enjoyed.

After saying goodbye to their friends, the couple headed downtown to the restaurant. All of Wynsome's senses heightened when she realized they were at the historic, romantic hotel.

"What are we doing here, Danny?"

"My parents recommended we try the restaurant here. They thought you would love it."

Right, Wynsome thought. *Maybe I don't need to do as much convincing as I thought I would. It seems like Danny is ready to take our relationship to the next level, too.*

Daniel handed his keys to his jeep to the valet and escorted Wynsome inside the restaurant. They sat at a romantic, dimly-lit table in the very back near a huge window. The sparkling lights and bare streets of the city looked serene. Letting loose a little, Daniel decided to share a bottle of champagne with Wynsome.

"Here is to the most beautiful, talented, intelligent woman I know. I am blessed to call you my girl. I pray we celebrate every one of your remaining birthdays together and as in love as we are now. Toast."

"That was beautiful. Do you really want us to last forever?"

"Forever, ever."

"I wonder if the rooms here are as lovely as this restaurant."

"I'm sure they are. My parents stayed here overnight celebrating the anniversary of their first date.

Can you believe they still do stuff like that? They loved it."

"I couldn't have asked for a better birthday."

"The evening is not over yet. We have another stop after dinner; after you try the cheesecake. I know how much you love cheesecake. My dad thinks theirs is the second best in the state of Alabama; his being the first, of course."

"You spoil me, Daniel. We better stay together forever because you have ruined me for anyone else. No one can top you."

"I'm thankful the Lord saw fit for me to meet you."

"I like the way you express your love. I can't wait to fully express my love to you."

"You've already shown me."

"Not like this." Wynsome leaned over the table and passionately kissed him.

"Wow," was all Daniel could manage to say.

"Maybe we should get a room," Wynsome said.

With a crumpled brow, Daniel reminded Wynsome, "I want to be with you just as much as you want to be with me, probably more, but we both agreed we were doing things the Lord's way. Just think about how good it will be because of our obedience."

Wynsome gave Daniel an eyeful as she leaned on the table and purred, "I think it's time to move to the next level. We both know God wants us to be together for the rest of our lives, and we will, right after graduation. Technically, there's really no need to wait."

With a strong, steady voice, Daniel replied, "I know it's hard, Wynsome. It's difficult for me, too, but the Holy Spirit will continue to help us withstand."

"Let's leave that super-spiritual talk alone for a minute and be real, it's just me and you here," no longer trying to mask her irritation.

"There is no me and you without Him. I love you, Wynsome, but I love Him more." Seeing the hurt on her face, Daniel added, "And you should, too. Let's table this for now and finish your birthday celebration."

"Okay."

They sat quietly and stared out the window as they waited for dessert to arrive.

"Guess where we are going next?" Daniel asked, trying to distract Wynsome from her anger. He knew how much she hated not getting her way.

"I have no idea." Wynsome had no interest in making this easy for Daniel.

They ate their dessert in silence. Wynsome just played around with hers. When they were done eating, she excused herself to the restroom while Daniel took care of the bill. Daniel searched his brain for something he could do to cheer Wynsome up. He had something in his pocket he was saving for the end of the night, but he decided to give it to her now.

When Wynsome exited the restroom, Daniel was down on one knee right outside of the bathroom door.

Wynsome looked at him as if he had lost his mind. "What are you doing on the floor, boy? Get up before someone sees you." The restaurant was empty except for one other couple.

Daniel pulled a ring box out of his pocket. "Wyni, you know you are the love of my life. This ring symbolizes how complete my love is for you. I promise I will always be here. Please accept this ring exemplifying my commitment. You will be my wife one day. It'll be worth the wait for me and you."

With a blank expression on her face, Wynsome just stared at the ring. She took the ring box out of his hand to get a closer look at it. Noticing the concern on Daniel's face, she continued her examination and took an even closer look after taking the ring out of the box.

When she felt she had tormented him enough, she squealed, "Of course, I do. This ring is beautiful. I will keep it close until the day we are officially engaged. You are the most wonderfullest guy in the world," she said with an extended kiss.

"And you are the most beautifullest woman in this world, inside and out."

As they walked out of the restaurant, Wynsome asked, "Where are we going next?"

The dance club they were headed to was just around the corner. When they entered, Wynsome immediately spotted everyone they had drinks with earlier dancing and having a good time. Wynsome didn't really have any female friends, but she was glad the ladies were there to share in her excitement. When they noticed Daniel and Wynsome had arrived, all the girls ran off to the nearest restroom so Wynsome could tell them all about the promise ring.

The guys did not wait for the girls to get back before joining everyone else on the dance floor doing the latest line dance. They did the bunny hop and the electric slide before the ladies returned. *They just saw each other about an hour ago. They couldn't have that much to talk about!* Daniel thought.

When the ladies finally returned they joined the guys on the floor. It wasn't too crowded or smoky in the club—just laid back and fun. About thirty people crowded the tiny club, and everybody was on the dance floor. In addition to the two cocktails Wynsome had before dinner and the glass of champagne at the hotel, she had a couple more drinks at the club. She was nice by the time they were ready to leave. It had been awhile since Daniel had seen Wynsome this inebriated. He practically had to carry her out the club.

After shutting the club down, Wynsome and Daniel said goodnight to their friends and headed back to campus. When he pulled up in front of Wynsome's dorm, he parked the car and escorted her to her private room. He told Wynsome goodnight and tried to leave after she was secure in her room, but she insisted he stay awhile. It was close to 2 a.m. He promised himself not to be alone with her after 10:00 p.m. to prevent ending up in tempting situations. But Wynsome looked like she might let go at any time all the cheesecake and cocktails she had. Against his better judgment, Daniel stayed to make sure she was okay.

"I'm going to get out of this dress and wash my face. Wait for me on the couch in the common area," Wynsome told Daniel.

Daniel went into the common area and turned on the television while he waited. He was so tired he began to nod off. Soon, the television was watching him.

Wynsome gently woke him when she returned, "Hey, sleepyhead, come in my room and lay down. Stay with me until I fall asleep. That cheesecake tasted great going down but not so much coming up. I'm going to get a glass of ginger ale then join you."

"It's really late, I should head back to my dorm. "

"Alright, Daniel," Wynsome said, trying to keep from retching. Daniel quickly located a trashcan and rushed to her aide. Gasping for air, she said, "There can't be anything else to come up. I released it all." Daniel instructed her to go lay down while he retrieved the ginger ale.

When Daniel entered the bedroom, Wynsome was tucked tightly in bed watching *Duck Dynasty*. He handed her the glass of soda, climbed in on the opposite side of the bed without turning down the blanket and watched with her. After Wynsome took a sip of the soda, she placed it on a coaster on her night stand. She scooted over and laid down with her head on Daniel's chest. She allowed her hands to roam all over his upper body. He enjoyed every stroke of her fingertips. Noticing Daniel wasn't stopping her, Wynsome continued and added a kiss on his forehead, then his mouth.

Their petting escalated and somehow Wynsome was no longer tucked under the blanket. She was on top of Daniel. Daniel glanced at the carpet covered with clothing, and realized they were both practically naked. Daniel heard a low still voice say his name. Daniel sat up immediately and gently placed Wynsome on the other side of the bed. As hard as it was for him to stop, he mustered up the will to tell Wynsome they shouldn't do this. Daniel dashed out of the bed, picked up all of his clothing, and ran into the bathroom. After putting on his clothes, he yelled, "I'll call you later," and ran out the door.

~~~

Rev. Ashley asked Jodie to meet her at a trendy eatery not too far from Church. When Jodie arrived, they sat on either side of a table made from an aged door and chairs made from old wooden movie theater seats. Jodie stared over her right shoulder through the picture window. *The young professionals walking their dogs must live in the nearby lofts,* she thought.

Rev. Ashley stared over her left shoulder trying to determine the relationship between the elderly homeless-looking black man playing chess with a little Asian girl at a table across from the cash register. She was baffled no one else seemed to be concerned about this. Instead, people were whispering about the young, overweight white guy sitting on the mourning bench against the wall with his bare feet propped up on the table in front of him. Just before he had made himself comfortable, a server had removed the remnants of a bacon, lettuce and fried green tomato sandwich recently abandoned by a Dominican nursing student.

Shaking her head, Rev. Ashley turned her attention to Jodie, "How are you doing?"

Still staring out the window, Jodie said "A little nervous."

Chuckling, Rev. Ashley responded, "You don't have to be afraid of me, girl. You know we aren't that far apart in age; we probably have a lot in common."

"Maybe," Jodie said highly doubtful.

"I'm sure we do. I enjoyed your poem; it was so heartfelt. I could feel your conflicting emotions as I read it. I must admit that I have been in similar situations myself."

"Oh really."

Here we go again with these one word answers, Rev. Ashley thought.

"Tell me more about this guy the poem is about. I assume it's about a man. Am I right? What's his name?"

Jodie finally looked Rev. Ashley directly in her face, "Yeah, you are right. His name is Amir. We actually met in the music production class I enrolled in when I first came home from college."

The first night of class, Jodie had sat in the front left side of the classroom. Amir, Jodie, and one other man were the only black people in the class of about twenty-five students. She studied Amir during break and found him to be very attractive but immediately ruled out the possibility of dating him because he appeared too macho, worldly, and street smart. Girls like her shouldn't date guys like him, and guys like him wouldn't be interested in her anyway.

He eventually grew on her though. He sat next to her the second week of class even though he had sat in the absolute back of the classroom the week before. The third week, he gave her his business card and suggested they get together. The fourth week, he drove her to her car after class. She had to park far away from their class building because of a football game in progress on the campus. He said he couldn't resist helping a woman in distress. They had been seeing each other ever since.

"From your poem, this Amir sounds like a charmer."

Shaking her head, "My main reason for taking that class was to try to stay out of trouble but I ran right into it when I met him."

"Is. . . this. . . a sexual relationship? "

"I'm not playing myself. I know this is not a real relationship. It is just about sex. Amir is not interested in committing to me. I call it a non-relationship."

Smirking, Rev. Ashley responded, "Is this the first non-relationship you have been in?"

"No. I've had one other; Patrick from church."

Rev. Ashley showed no reaction. "Is that the wrong thing you thought you would never do? You never thought you would get involved in something like that, didn't you?"

"Yeah. I was a tease in high school. I didn't think there was anything wrong with it and still planned to remain a virgin until marriage. But during my senior year in college, many of the young men in the campus ministry fellowship I was a part of said they would only marry 'real' virgins and not this born again virgin stuff that's been going around in Christian circles."

"Why did that bother you? You were still a virgin."

"I didn't feel like one," Jodie answered, forlorn.

"That's why we can't go by our feelings, girl. Our feelings don't necessarily reflect reality. Satan used those comments made by your Christian brothers to make you feel unclean and unholy."

"Well, he got me," Jodie said, taking a deep breath.

"The devil took the opportunity to convince you to go ahead and do it because you had already gone so far."

Nodding, "That's exactly the way I felt," Jodie said.

"Don't allow your feelings to dictate whether or not you are holy. Believe you are holy even when you don't feel like it because the One who lives inside you is holy."

"That makes a lot of sense and sounds real good, but exactly how do I do that?"

"It will take a lot of work. You will have to be willing to give all your hurts, disappointments, and desires to God. You will have to make a commitment and God will take care of the rest. He'll even help you make the commitment."

~~~

There was nothing else for Xavier to do in his jail cell but think. He tried reading the Bible Mr. Roberts gave him, but found it difficult to understand. He tried praying but only got frustrated. The more time he spent alone, the more he doubted himself.

Thinking about Michelle took up most of his time. He and Michelle had become a couple soon after attending that birthday party together. Things had escalated quickly. They had begun living together in

Michelle's condo and entertained the idea of getting married one day.

The true test of their relationship came when Michelle found out she was pregnant. She was depressed and angry with herself for letting Xavier talk her into breaking her double-up rule: birth control and a condom every time. Xavier was also upset because he didn't want any more kids, but he had never bothered to share that with Michelle.

Xavier pleaded with Michelle not to keep the baby, but Michelle refused and she took him to court to get a child support agreement as soon as it was possible. Their relationship had no chance at survival and all their love dissipated. Xavier thought to himself: *I never understood why men are financially responsible to help take care of a child they insisted on not having. Women want the right to choose, but when they choose to have a child on their own, they don't want to take care of the child on their own.*

Xavier began to resent Michelle and refused to spend any time with Miller, but he kept running into them at his mother's house. His mother refused to hold his grudge. With his mother's coaxing, Xavier eventually overcame his bitterness and developed a relationship with his son but in the back of his mind, he never forgave Michelle for keeping the baby. Her decision made his life more difficult. Now, he would always have to struggle to make ends meet.

Xavier started to seriously question his actions the night Michelle got shot. Her aunt and uncle seemed to sincerely believe it was an accident, but he wasn't sure anymore. After all, the pregnancy news did have him fuming and Michelle's pointed insults heated him up even more. She knew exactly how to push his buttons and when to push them.

Xavier was emotionally spent. He crawled into one of the cell's four corners, balled up in the fetal position and cried until his face was raw.

~~~

To: Rev.J.Ashley@church.org
From: J_Sutton@southerntraditionsmail.com
Subject: Another Again

Hey. I got your voice message and . . . umm. . . I wasn't avoiding you. Okay, I was. And yes . . . It's because I saw Amir again. I know you suggested I not see 'Splenda' again after I told you about that horrible night. I'm still tripping over that nickname you gave him. It fits, though, because I hate sugar substitutes and our non-relationship is a poor substitute for a real one.

He tried to come to my house, but I promised myself I would never let him in my home again after he made me feel so unsafe in it that night. So we met at that soul food restaurant off Finley Ave, instead. I had been doing well and was convinced he had no chance of talking me into something I had already made a commitment not to do. This was one of the few times sex was not involved in our visit.

We had a nice, flirty chat even though he tried bringing up that night, but I reminded him we decided to never speak of that ever again.

You won't believe this! He is moving to New York in three weeks to pursue his screenwriting career. He has saved up enough money and sold most of his material possessions to make it happen. He's always said he was working on moving, but I never took him seriously.

I admire him for that, though, going after his dreams. I wish I were that confident and bold to quit my job and pursue my passion (I don't rightly know what that is, though) full time. I wished him the best of luck and told him I thought it would be best that we didn't keep in touch, and he agreed.

When we stood at our cars saying goodbye, he hugged me tightly. His embrace was very firm and familiar, but not a good kind of familiar. This familiar made me feel afraid. Feelings arose in me that I didn't like feeling, those same feelings I had that horrible night. My paranoia prompted me to look around and make sure there were bystanders in case I needed some help. As quickly as the emotions came, they left. It was very jarring, but I recovered quickly.

Anyway, the Lord is so good to me! I just prayed this morning for the Lord to help me leave Amir alone and what does He do? He loves me so much to move Amir all the way across the country so I can't have ready access to him. God knows I'm not strong enough to resist him while he is in the same state as me. PTL!!

J. Sutton

~~~

Rev. Ashley called a special session of Truthseekers to pray for Michelle and her family. Michelle's hospital stay has lasted longer than expected. The prayer meeting was open to the entire congregation and community. When Wynsome arrived, she found they had moved from their regular meeting space to the sanctuary because so many people had showed up. That was a good sign.

A couple people from the worship team led them in a couple of impromptu songs, a cappella.

When they finished setting the atmosphere, Rev. Ashley explained her vision for the prayer meeting.

"Church, we are here to left up the Roberts family in prayer. They have experienced an unexpected tragedy that affects the lives of many people. As the body of Christ and their church family, it is our obligation and responsibility to keep them lifted up in continuous prayer.

So, while I pray aloud I want you to pray where you are in any way you are led. The Holy Spirit is in control, and He doesn't move the same in every person. So, do what you do. Pray silently or aloud. You may feel led to moan or sing, kneel, or stand. Pray in your native tongue or in your heavenly language."

Wynsome felt consumed by a heavy spirit she couldn't explain and had never felt before. All of this was new to her. Daniel wasn't there to guide and explain it to her as he normally does. He is gifted with the ability to break these spiritual things down in laymen's terms. She convinced herself to stop worrying about what others were doing and do what she was there to do. Michelle really needed all the prayers she could get.

For about an hour, some people knelt at the altar and prayed while others walked through every pew mouthing words. Some sat in one spot and rocked back and forth, moaning. There were a group of women in the foyer speaking aloud in a gibberish only God could understand.

Rev. Ashley lifted from her position of laying prostrate in the aisle to share something with the congregation. She was hard to understand because was hoarse and naturally spoke softly anyway.

"The Holy Spirit has led me to give a brief Word tonight. I know this is not what we planned, but as I said from the beginning, the Holy Spirit is in control."

"I keep hearing the phrase 'When I Move, You Move (just like that).'

With what Daniel calls her ugly face plastered on, Wynsome said to herself, *Is she sure that was the Holy Spirit speaking to her or was she listening to the old school hip-hop channel on her way to church tonight because that's the title of a Ludacris song.*

"Numbers, Chapter 9 talks about the Tent of Agreement. The tent was set up with a cloud covering it. From dusk until dawn, the cloud above the tent looked like fire. The Israelites kept a close watch on the cloud that hung above the tent. When the cloud moved, the Israelites moved. If the cloud didn't move, they stayed camped in that same place. Sometimes the cloud stayed over the tent for a short time, a month, or a year. No matter the time of day, the Israelites moved when the cloud moved. They camped as long as the cloud stayed. The Israelites obeyed the Lord and looked to Him for direction.

As children of God, we should be just like the Israelites in this passage. We should be like sheep following our shepherd. Our focus should always be on God. We should always be in a position of expectation.

We can't be caught trying to get ready when God decides to move. We must stay ready. Keep your lamps trimmed and burning. Keep plenty of extra oil. We shouldn't waste time mulling it over, trying to rationalize it. When God moves, we move. If God isn't moving, we wait expectantly for His next move.

We have to be dependent on God. The world teaches us to be selfish and to be concerned only about ourselves. I-N-D-E-P-E-N-D-E-N-T. . .do you know what that means? Yes Church, another secular song reference, but I know most of y'all know the lyrics. The song says she got her own house, her own car, has two jobs, and works hard. The only time she needs a man is for. . .you know. But anytime we start to think that we have all these things by our own volition, we deceive ourselves. He blessed us with these things and the good health to enjoy them. Believing and/or trying to live independently of God is sin."

Deacon Rouser stood at the back of the church looking disapprovingly at his daughter. *This child cannot be mine, having this congregation speaking in tongues and all that. We didn't do all that growing up. She may be grown, but she better remember where she came from and respect her daddy and this church's traditions. She is not going to embarrass me!*

Rev. Ashley continued, "When God moves, we should move. When God speaks, we should listen and obey. When God convicts, we should repent and get back up again. Just like that. It's that simple, but we try to make it so hard. We must deny our flesh, walk in the Spirit, and keep our eyes focused on God."

Now Rev. Ashley had to know, Ludacris' lyrics are too harsh and demeaning for church, Webbie's lyrics, too. But her on the spot message was on point, Wynsome thought.

As the prayer warriors exited the sanctuary, Rev. Ashley made eye contact with her dad. They hardly ever talked other than to discuss the declining health of her grandmother. But at that moment, Rev. Ashley felt convicted to go talk to him. Even though exasperated, she was clear of what God wanted her to do. Her original plan to go back to her office after the prayer meeting and enjoy a Buffalo Rock in silence had been shattered.

When Deacon Rouser saw her walking in his direction, she noticed him looking around for a quick escape but he was blocked on every side. A group of their hearing impaired members were having a lively conversation with their hands right in front of him, and he was surrounded on every remaining side by teenagers planning their next social outing.

Really God, do I have to do this? Do I have to do it now? How about I call him later? I don't want to talk to this man, and obviously he doesn't want to talk to me. It takes so much energy to deal with him, Rev. Ashley thought as she wrestled with the Holy Spirit.

When Rev. Ashley finally reached Deacon Rouser, they gave each other a lukewarm greeting.

"It's good to see you, Dad."

"Umph," Deacon Rouser grumbled.

Both of them welcomed Oneilia Sutton's interruption of their bland exchange when she broke through the crowd to reach them.

"Deacon, I know you have to be proud of how much your only child has grown in her relationship with God. She is such a blessing to our young people."

"Umph. Seems like she is just stirring up trouble to me."

"How so?" Rev. Ashley inquired.

Deacon Rouser kept his glare on Oneilia. "She was not taught to conduct herself like that when she was growing up in this church. She know we do things the right way; in decency and in order.

"In what way am I conducting myself, Daddy?" Rev. Ashley said raising her already soft voice. She hated it that he wouldn't speak directly to her; almost like he didn't find her worthy of his respect.

"Oneilia, your daughter Jodie knows we do not speak in tongues during a church service unless there is immediate interpretation, right?"

"That is how they were taught, Ruben. What is your point?

"Did that happen here tonight?"

"Well, your daughter did share a word from the Lord after all the prayers had been made."

"You know that's not how it works, Oneilia. One person speaks in tongues, someone else interprets right after. There is a structure to these things."

"Daddy, why are you talking about me like I'm not even here? You can answer my questions directly to me."

"Oneilia, I don't know where she has gotten this mess from. Probably from that mega church her mom took her to in Nashville. That's why her mother and I didn't work out. She wanted to break all the traditions."

I'm not going to waste my breath arguing with this fool. It is not worth getting my pressure worked up, Oneilia mused to herself.

Deacon Rouser spotted a clear path to escape and swiftly walked away, mumbling, "She is not going to come in here corrupting our children with this neo, pseudo-charismatic stuff endorsed by televangelists. Looking like the world, using worldly song lyrics in the sanctuary. Just blasphemous!"

Why couldn't I just have had a Buffalo Rock, God? Why? Rev. Ashley prayed as she stood in the middle of the foyer with Mrs. Sutton dumbfounded.

‖‖ ‖‖‖

Carol sat in Michelle's hospital room as Nurse Collins assisted Michelle out of bed and to the restroom for a bath. Michelle grimaced in pain. When they were in the privacy of the restroom, Nurse Collins drummed up the courage to ask Michelle a question that had been on her mind.

"You must be really angry at the person who did this to you."

"Not so much, no. I'm just thankful God allowed me to survive. I'm sure Xavier is in worse shape than I am with his freedom hanging in the balance. I've found my freedom no matter where my body may end up. I pray this situation will help Xavier see he needs to stop playing with God before it's too late and get in right relationship. My current circumstances sure 'nuff brought me closer to God."

"Why aren't you mad with God? Shoot, I'm mad at Him for you. God allowed this to happen to you."

"God also brought me through it. I have faith that He will work this situation out for my good. I know that you don't see much good right now. I don't either, but let me tell you, my new understanding of God is enough for me to keep hope alive."

"Wow! You're starting to sound like you been saved, for real."

"Even though I just gave my life to Christ a few days ago, my family laid a good foundation. All their talk about the church, God, and Christ finally started making sense to me. My aunt and uncle lived an uncompromising life in front of my cousin Daniel and I came along. Don't get me wrong, they aren't perfect, but they let us see their imperfections so we could really see the need for Jesus. It had to take me almost losing my life for me to realize how empty life is without Him," Michelle said as if she was talking to herself.

After the bath, the nurse carefully walked Michelle back to her bed and got her settled in for the night. Carol was already asleep in the chair when Michelle drifted off.

Around 1 a.m., Carol started stirring in her sleep. Something in her spirit told her to get up, but sleep felt too good to her. She was awakened again by loud sounds in the hospital room. As she began to wake up, she realized the monitors attached to Michelle were screeching. Nurses ran into the room. "What's going on?" Carol exclaimed.

"Michelle's blood pressure is dropping quickly and her pulse is beating rapidly. We can't get her to wake up. It appears her body is going into v-tach. We are going to have to ask you to step outside the room, ma'am," the overnight nurse instructed.

Carol stepped outside the room. A nurse's aide accompanied her for support. Carol immediately started praying and speaking in tongues while pacing up and down the corridor. All of a sudden, she stopped in her tracks and a peaceful look came over her face.

"Why did you stop?" the nurse's aide asked.

"Because the Lord spoke to my spirit."

"Sho 'nuff? What He say?" the nurse's aide asked with her hands on her hips.

"He said my child is now with me, safe in my hands."

The overnight nurse came out of the room with a gloomy look on her face. "I'm sorry, Mrs. Roberts, but we were unable to revive her. It appears she had some internal bleeding. We performed CPR, but it didn't work. Time of death- 2:14 a.m."

~~~

After making Michelle's final funeral arrangements, the Roberts dropped off Miller and Michelle's father, Bernard, at his house. They crashed when they got home, relieved the busy and stressful day was over. Carol had forgotten everything entailed in settling a person's affairs. The whole process was exhausting and wearing everyone thin.

Immediately after entering the house and putting down her purse in a nearby chair, Carol went to the kitchen to prepare dinner. All she had to do was warm up one of the many casseroles the ladies from Church had graciously prepared for them. As she put together a salad to accompany the chicken, broccoli, rice, and cheese casserole, Daniel walked in searching for a bottle of water.

"Are you sure you'll be able to hold it together long enough to do the eulogy, Daniel? Your emotions may get in the way. Maybe Pastor Longhorn should do it. You should have an opportunity to grieve properly," Carol suggested while she cut up the tomatoes for the salad.

"Mom, Michelle rarely went to church, so Pastor Longhorn will only know what we tell him anyway. I want to do it because I can give people a glimpse of the real Michelle. I thank God He allowed me to witness her conversion before her death. Now, I am sure I'll see her again. I really thought she was going to pull through, Mom. I didn't think her life would end."

Carol stopped putting the final touches on their dinner to comfort Daniel with a quick embrace. Suddenly Daniel froze.

"Mom, where is Dad?'

"I don't know. Come to think about it, I haven't seen him since we got home." Carol wiped her hands on a nearby dishtowel, handed it to Daniel and left the kitchen to go find her husband. She found him crying on the side of the jetted tub in the master bathroom. Carol couldn't keep from breaking down in tears when she saw him in so much emotional pain. She walked into the bathroom, sat awkwardly on the side of the tub, and held him tight as if the force would heal all his hurts. When his sobs quieted, Carol led him into the bedroom and they sat down on their queen-sized bed. She held Paul and prayed silently for their family to get through this storm unscathed.

Breaking the silence, Carol assured Paul he was not alone.

"Michelle is biologically our niece, but my daughter in my heart. Why did God take Michelle away so soon after giving her life to Christ? Why didn't God let her baby girl live?" Paul said.

116

"I don't have a clue," Carol shrieked throwing up her hands in despair. Paul stared at her in utter disbelief. She is usually the cool-headed one.

"What?" Carol demanded. "You want me to lie about how I feel and give you all the perfect super spiritual answers? Tell you count it all joy and we'll understand it better by and by? Well, we may never understand this. But we have to trust God is who He says He is. Shoot, He better show his face soon before I lose *my* mind! That's all I'm saying. Now, go on in that bathroom, clean up, and meet us downstairs for dinner. Daniel was getting worried about you."

Finally, the family sat down at the same time for the first time in a long time and used the opportunity to take care of important family matters.

"Do. . .do. . . you think we should raise Miller?" Carol probed.

"I don't see any other option," answered Paul.

"Today I heard Uncle Bernard mention retiring to raise Miller," Daniel chimed in.

"Bernard hasn't raised anything other than his hands his whole life. And that was to ask for money. He's trying to atone for missing out on Michelle's childhood. I'm sure Xavier would want us to take on the responsibility and so would Michelle," Carol assured the men.

"The question is, do you two have the stamina to raise a young boy?" Daniel said bringing up a good point.

"We *are* getting older, Danny. We can't juggle as many responsibilities as we used to and keep a child happy. So we would be counting on you to help as well," his father said sternly.

"Okay, sure, I'll help with the kid. But remember, I'm still a kid, too. I'll be on your insurance until I'm at least twenty-six, thanks to President Obama,"
Daniel said mischievously.

Rolling her eyes at Daniel, "If we do raise him, we must make sure he keeps a relationship with his dad, sister, brothers, and Bernard," Carol said.

"And we will make sure he knows all the lovely memories of his mother," Paul said.

Excitedly, Daniel started to reminisce, "Remember when Xavier finally decided he wanted to have a relationship with Miller but Michelle was still sour? To get her attention, Xavier paid his child support all in dimes and gave it to her in a Crown Royal bag. I still can't believe he came up with that all on his own."

"That was funny," Paul said as he chuckled heartily.

"Paul! There's nothing amusing about that," Carol declared indignantly as the men continued to laugh at the memory.

~~~

The Larsen and Roberts families, along with other family members, friends, and acquaintances, gathered at the church to celebrate the life and love of Michelle Ashlynn Larsen. Carol and Bernard selected a lovely antique gold coffin and beautiful white suit for Michelle to wear. Michelle lay peacefully in the casket with a picture of Miller on her chest. She always made sure her little man was well taken care of. Michelle left her personal affairs in order. She had made sure her life insurance policy would cover the cost of her funeral, the complete payoff of her condo, and any medical expenses. Her will explained if anything were to ever happen to her and Xavier, Miller should be raised by her aunt and uncle. If they were not available, then Daniel would be his guardian. Miller's higher education was already paid for because she had a college fund set up for him.

As the services began, a male soloist opened with the powerful anthem "You are God Alone," reminding everyone of who was really in control. After the soloist, Deacon Odell King read the Old and New Testament scriptures. Family friends and schoolmates offered tributes and fond memories before Daniel gave the eulogy.

First, he dried his eyes and cleared his throat. He contemplated wearing dark sunglasses to conceal his emotions like he had seen many people do at funerals, but the Holy Spirit spoke to him and told him to allow God to be his protector because you never know, your vulnerability may set someone else free. Daniel decided today was as good a day as any to obey the Holy Spirit.

"I've been to many funerals in my life. I've listened to preachers talk about people they barely knew, recalling the few encounters, if any, they had with the deceased or maybe only tearful memories the family shared with them. Or the preacher spoke just plain ole, made-up stuff, a life the deceased's family wished their loved one had lived.

Allow me to share my personal memories of Michelle. She was outright rebellious growing up but looked after me as any big sister would. She eventually matured into a wonderful person, a responsible mom, and successful entrepreneur but not without some trial and error of course. Even though she was a single mom, she took responsibility for her actions, didn't blame anyone, didn't believe the world owed her something for nothing, and did what was necessary to care for her son. She was strong-willed, intelligent, and stubborn. Maybe that's why I date girls with the same qualities; Daniel said with a chuckle, smiling in Wynsome's direction.

I was there when Michelle gave her life to the Lord. She did it just hours before she died. She handled her new circumstances graciously and focused on getting better. I don't have to lie and tell you she is in heaven right now because I know she is. I'm not going to lie and say you will see her again. That part is actually up to you. Make the choice Michelle made. Michelle didn't know her life was going to end hours later, and you don't know what's in store for your future. Take the hand of the Savior who loves you who does know what's ahead.

Do you want to spend eternity with Him? Death is final. Michelle is not coming back. All people who die will not see God. Do you have blessed assurance today you will one day see Him? If not, come down and give your life to the Lord. Do not let Michelle's death be in vain. My mother told me Michelle ministered to one of her nurses the day she died, not knowing that was going to be her last opportunity to share her faith. Even though she is not physically with us anymore, her life can still produce fruit through her death. If you are saved, are you using your faith to help others? I'm no preacher. I am just trying to walk out this Jesus lifestyle. I offer you the same opportunity. Get saved for real.

Silent tears washed down Daniel's face. He turned and left the pulpit. Pastor Longhorn got up and offered an invitation to Christian discipleship. One by one, many people went down the aisle to give their lives to the Lord. Daniel recognized several nurses from University come forward including Nurse Collins. Miller and Bernard also gave their lives to the Lord that day.

People gasped loudly when Xavier appeared at the altar. He came in like a ghost undetected. Many of the bereaved questioned aloud his audacity showing up at Michelle's funeral and couldn't believe he was released from jail to come. They later found out the judge had served on the police force with Xavier's boss before going to law school and granted him a temporary reprieve to attend. That was a miracle; that judge rarely gave such privileges. To everyone else's surprise, Paul and Daniel were ecstatic to see him.

Carol stood next to Miller and Bernard for support so Paul got up and stood beside Xavier. Pastor Longhorn prayed the prayer of salvation with all the people who joined him at the altar. When he finished, he invited the new converts to connect with the spiritual advisors in the fellowship hall for personal prayer.

~~~

Daniel was emotionally exhausted from the day's events. He needed to get away from the many people hanging around his parents' house. He readily accepted Wynsome's suggestion to go back to campus with her until the crowd cleared.

When Daniel parked in front of Wynsome's dorm, they sat there for a while before wandering silently around campus. They finally rested on the dorm's front stoop.

Laying her head on his shoulder, Wynsome whispered, "I know it's been a tough day for you. Do you want to talk about it? I know all of this must weigh seriously on you."

"I'm really tired. My mind is so hazy right now, I can't think straight. There are so many things to prepare for. I haven't had a chance to tell you yet, but I'm moving off campus at the end of the semester."

"Why? Where?"

"Michelle left me her condo."

"You don't think it will creep you out to live in her space with her gone—the place where she was shot by her son's father?"

"I think it's a good idea to keep it in the family for Miller's sake. He can hang out with me at the home he lived in with his mother anytime. Anyway, the loft has been so thoroughly cleaned and sanitized, there is no hint that a murder ever occurred there."

"Okay, if you are sure you can handle it. I am so proud of you. Your eulogy made a huge impact. I can't believe all those people came up at the end of the service."

"We usually don't invite people to Christian discipleship at funerals, but it just felt like it was the right thing to do. There is even life in death." Sighing loudly, Daniel continued, "I don't think I can hang much longer. Let's get you inside. I need to head back to the house. I hope that no one will see me when I get there. I don't want to talk to another mourner."

"Stay on campus with me tonight. You don't have to go back to that madhouse right now."

"That is not a good idea. I'll make sure you get in safely then I'll be on my way."

As soon as they walked into Wynsome's suite, she removed her suit jacket to reveal a lacy camisole. She took off her uncomfortable but fierce pumps, exposing her pretty feet. Daniel had had a thing for pretty feet for as long as he could remember. Noticing his thoughts beginning to wander, he walked close to Wynsome and leaned in to kiss her goodbye. He gave her a peck on her mouth and turned towards the door, but Wynsome gently turned him so he faced her.

"Can I have one more kiss," Wynsome purred.

She gave him a series of small pecks on the mouth, cheek, and forehead then back to his mouth allowing her lips to linger there longer while seductively biting his bottom lip. Daniel hadn't experienced anything like that before. He tried to resist her as she led him to the couch. Wynsome laid on his chest, skin to skin and Daniel wrapped his arms around her. Daniel was relieved and disappointed at the same time when the kisses stopped. They both lay still, enjoying the embrace and eventually falling asleep.

Daniel woke up disoriented and not conscious of his whereabouts. He looked down, saw Wynsome sleeping peacefully and remembered he was in her dorm room.

When she began to stir, she growled, "Your parents have probably sent a search wagon out for you."

"Whoa. Clear that frog out your throat. You're joking, but that's probably the truth. I was too tired and too comfortable to leave last night. Uh oh . . . this is my mom calling now."

Daniel groggily answered the phone, "Hello."

"Good Morning, Daniel Bernstein Roberts. How are you this morning?

Uh oh. I'm really in trouble if she is using that horrible middle name grandma gave me. "I'm fine, Mom. What about you?" Daniel answered as if this was going to be any normal conversation.

"I'm glad you asked. Well, after taking my morning shower, combing my hair, and getting dressed, I looked in your room to see if you were awake. I was dumbfounded when I saw your bed appeared untouched. I didn't know whether to be angry or worried. Now you tell me, which one should I be?"

"Don't worry, Mom. When I brought Wynsome back to campus last night, I fell asleep on her couch. I'm heading home now." He decided to go ahead and tell the truth.

"Okay. You are talking fast, so I'm not sure if that is the complete truth. I'll have breakfast waiting for you when you get here." That meant, *hurry up and get your butt home.*

Thank you, Lord, for protecting me from falling into sin even though I continue to put myself in tempting situations. I don't want to ruin what Wynsome and I have and I want to honor you, Daniel prayed on his way out of the door.

~~~

Carol started breakfast with her mind more on Daniel and Wynsome than the task in front of her. She's done this so often, though; she could probably cook breakfast half asleep. When she thought about it, she was convinced that she actually had done it half asleep at some point. The smells wafted up the stairs and woke Paul from a restless sleep. Pulling a shirt over his head, Paul slid his feet in his monogramed slippers Miller gave him for Christmas; one said, "Paw" and the other said, "Paul". When completely dressed, he walked briskly down the stairs to get the best piece of bacon. He liked his extra crispy and real pork instead of that turkey bacon Carol tried to sneak in sometimes.

"Good morning, honey," Paul said as he leaned over and kissed his wife on the cheek. "I'm surprised Daniel didn't beat me down here with this food filling the house with smell-goods."

"Good morning, sweetheart. Daniel stayed with Wynsome last night."

"What you talking 'bout, woman?" he said in a weak Diff'rent Strokes Gary Coleman impersonation as he fixed himself a cup of coffee.

"I called his cell when I figured out he never came home last night. He admitted he stayed overnight with Wynsome. You need to talk with your son before he takes a step he can't take back," Carol warned, looking at Paul from the corner of her eye.

"Why are you looking at me like that? Seriously, he is a grown man, and we can't control his comings and goings anymore. All we can do is pray he makes the best choices."

"You can also continue to guide him and hold him accountable."

Daniel walked in to see his parents in a heated discussion. When they noticed him, their attention quickly turned to him. *Dang!*

~~~

To: J_Sutton@southerntraditionsmail.com
From: Rev.J.Ashley@church.org
Subject: Never Again

You don't have to avoid me when you think you have messed up. I'm here to help keep you accountable. But most importantly, don't avoid God during those times. That's how we mess up, thinking we can fix ourselves before going before God again. But we can't be fixed until we go to God again.

Let me tell you, I ran into an old childhood friend from middle school this weekend in the parking lot of the grocery store off of HWY 31. All the mean things she had done to me in school flooded my brain. She told everyone I was gay, I only bathed once a month, and that I had a crush on her brother and stalked him. When I saw her, I went on and on about my accomplishments because I knew from the grapevine that she was single and unemployed with three kids and three trifling baby daddies. I got pleasure from watching her turn red from discomfort and embarrassment. When I got in the car, I had to repent though for trying to make her feel small and hurt her feelings all because of how she treated me over 20 years ago. We all mess up sometimes, even me.☐

I'm glad to hear Splenda has gone far, far away. Now you can use this time to explore why you fall into these kinds of relationships. Could it be low self-esteem?

Have you been reading the book I suggested in Truthseekers, *Victory over Darkness*? An exercise that helped me may help you. After I read the book, I listed on index cards scriptures that describe who I am in Christ and studied them. Another good exercise is to write all your negative feelings and thoughts about yourself on one side of a card then write on the other side what God says about you in that area.

You are making good progress, girl. I am proud of you!

Rev. Ashley

~~~

Rev. Ashley thought the young adults should experience the reward of giving back to the community, so the members of Truthseekers agreed to volunteer at the annual homeless community event at the downtown civic center, but only Jodie showed up. Rev. Ashley texted her saying she had a family issue to take care of so she would be about an hour late. Her grandmother had a rough night at the nursing home.

When Jodie entered the arena, there was an array of booths offering public assistance, health, and legal services. She was assigned the task of accompanying one client at a time to all the services they needed. When Jodie went to the door of the arena to meet her first client, she noticed a line of people two blocks long waiting to enter. Thankfully, there were folding chairs to sit in for people with special needs, the elderly, and expecting mothers.

Jodie was shocked by the sight of a woman who looked to be around eight month's pregnant leaning against a concrete wall in a yellow ill-fitting tank top smoking a cigarette. While Jodie mused in her disgust, one of the event coordinators walked up and delivered Jodie's first charge.

"Good Morning," Jodie said, "My name is Jodie. What would you like to have help with first today?"

"Hi, young lady. I am Ms. Weiss, and I need a new pair of dentures. These I have slip out without a moment's notice. That is so embarrassing. Do you think someone here can help me with that?" Ms. Weiss was a tiny woman with short, wiry, thin, white hair. She wore a dingy gray shift dress and black crocs with frog pins in the openings.

"We do have a mobile dental office right over here. Let's go see what your options are," Jodie answered. They hitched a ride on a golf cart shuttle and headed for the mobile dental care center first. It was stationed in the parking lot of the new entertainment district.

Ms. Weiss asked many questions in her deep scruffily voice on the short ride over.

"How did you get involved with this program—through your job? What do you do for a living?"

Jodie pointed to her royal blue polo shirt with the name and the address of her church on it, "I'm here representing my church, not my job, but I work for a company called Southern Traditions."

"What kind of church name is 'Church'?" Ms. Weiss asked as she examined Jodie's shirt but didn't wait for an answer. She rambled on, "Progress in the South is a noble idea, forget about the traditions. That sounds like very important work. What did you study at the University?"

Jodie looked around to see if anyone else was in earshot of this progressively interesting conversation, "I majored in marketing. I work in the sales department."

Standing at 4'11", Ms. Weiss picked imaginary lint from Jodie's shirt as she talked "Oh. You must be a smart young lady. Where is your husband?"

"I don't have one. I'm not married," Jodie said with her nose in the air.

"You were supposed to snag a husband along with that degree, honey."

"What? No one told me that! I guess I missed that opportunity."

"Well, that's what graduate schools are for. You may not have to go into more debt though because that young man over there with the camera has snapped many pictures of you. He's either smitten or a stalker. I'll let you figure that out," Ms. Weiss said, walking up the steps into the dental center, which was set up in one of the RVs used to house various medical and social services during the event. To protect their clients' privacy, all volunteers waited outside for them while they received their services.

The guy Ms. Weiss was referring to approached Jodie, just as Ms. Weiss disappeared into the RV. When she noticed his press pass, Jodie became very intrigued.

"You handled that little old lady well. My name is Wade Johnson," he reached out to shake her hand.

"Wayne?"

Throwing his head back with a chuckle he replied, "I get that all the time. No, not Wayne, it's Wade. Like the old negro spiritual."

"Oh, okay. I'm Jodie Sutton."

Ms. Weiss started walking down the steps of the dental center trailer. Wade knew he had to make his move fast. He didn't want to miss this opportunity. "Hey, here is my business card. I just moved to Birmingham from Atlanta, and I could use a friend in the area. Give me a call." Jodie agreed and handed him her business card before saying goodbye and taking Ms. Weiss to the legal services table.

As they stood in the long line, Jodie asked Ms. Weiss why she needed legal services. Ms. Weiss went into this long diatribe about how she ended up in Alabama. Another volunteer noticed she could barely stand on her feet and brought Ms. Weiss a chair. She sat down and told Jodie all about her childhood in Israel, her native country. She shared that she had lived in Egypt for a while before her daughter sent for her, bringing her to the United States. After living in Birmingham for six months with her daughter, her daughter put her out because Ms. Weiss did not get along with her boyfriend. A nice family from her daughter's church took her in for three months but eventually couldn't afford for her to continue to stay. Now she lived in a group home and needed an official I.D. to get public assistance.

"So, I just told you my life story. Now tell me about your troubles," Ms. Weiss said.

In a whisper, Jodie said, "As I think about it, I really don't have any troubles."

Whether he was awake or attempting sleep, Xavier couldn't keep the roaring whispers and slaughtering stares of Michelle's mourners from replaying in his mind. Xavier had asked God's forgiveness and, according to His Word, he had received it, but he couldn't shake the feeling that he deserved their hatred and an eternity in Hell. He tried to counter that memory with the words Pastor Longhorn had given him after the service. During the minister's personal counseling time, Pastor gave his full attention to Xavier. He had cautioned that even though a noticeably heavy load had been lifted off Xavier when he walked down that aisle, there would still be times when he wouldn't feel saved. This was one of those times.

The more and more he thought about it, the less Xavier was convinced that shooting Michelle had been an accident. She did say some nasty things and hit way below the belt. Michelle had not even considered his point of view. That did not give him an excuse to allow the situation to get out of hand, though. As a cop, he had been trained how to use a gun, trained to keep the safety on. But the situation that developed with Michelle was intensely personal and all that he knew had failed him.

He disregarded all the things he tried to teach his sons about treating a woman right and the standards he taught his daughter to accept from men. Now his life was over and he had ruined his children's lives as well. What would happen to Miller with his mother buried in Elmwood Cemetery and his father in prison for putting her there?

Mr. Roberts had assured Xavier during his last phone call that Michelle didn't have any animosity towards him when she died. Now, he needed to figure out how to forgive himself, pick up the pieces, and be useful with the rest of his life, even if it was behind bars.

A puzzling look crossed Xavier's face when he saw a guard unlocking the door to his cell and announced he had visitors. He was surprised to see Mr. Roberts, Daniel, and Deacon Odell King. They hugged him before sitting down on benches that belonged in an outdoor courtyard.

Daniel continuously looked over his shoulder while greeting Xavier as if it was crucial for him to watch his back.

"How are you doing, son," Mr. Roberts asked.

"I'm still here. How is Miller doing," Xavier inquired.

"He is maintaining. We hear him cry out in his sleep at night; calling for his mother. He isn't quite ready to come visit you yet. That's understandable. It's going to take some time. Mrs. Roberts and Bernard are doing well, considering."

Mr. Roberts didn't know what else to say to Xavier, so he joined the conversation Deacon King and Daniel were having to the side. Xavier zoned out, thinking about the damage he may have done to his son. He silently thanked God for the Roberts. Any other family would have crucified him for killing their loved one, no matter how close they were before the crime, but the Roberts had stood by his side throughout this whole ordeal. That alone proved God's love because he didn't think anyone could do that without the help of The Most High God.

Xavier started to weep, which caught the men off guard, "I can't tell you how grateful I am to have your love and support. Even though you are grieving and I am the cause of your grief, you are still thinking about me. Thank you for that. I don't know how you keep from hating me. Sometimes I think I hate me."

"Xavier, you have always been family to us and you will always be family. Family sticks together. Frankly, son, only the Holy Spirit can maintain a love like this because I sho' nuff wanted to hate you. I won't lie," Paul added with a chuckle. Xavier gave a smile and a nod, knowing exactly where Paul was coming from.

"They only allowed us to come visit with you for a short while. Odell, will you lead us in prayer before we leave? That guard over there is eyeing us hard right now. Xavier, we will always be here for you because you are God's son and you are Miller's father."

"Let's pray," Deacon King said as he bowed his head.

Oh dear gracious God. Thank ya for bringing us together today. Please forgive each one of us all sins committed by thought, word, or deed. Help us to live tha life free from sin that can over take us if we let it. We don't want to die 'cause of our sinful ways, Lawd.

Please bring comfort and peace to our brother Xavier. Send him the best legal counsel this system got to offer to help him get out of this here mess he got himself in. We pray for the health of his mind. We pray he will rely on You for his strenfth, Lawd. We end this prayer claiming for ya perfect will to be done during the trial. Pray the attorneys and judge operate in integrity. Pray ya wisdom and will be done. Hear me, Lawd, thy will be done. Where our will don't line up wit' yours, whip it in line 'til it does. In Jesus name. Amen."

~~~

During the ride home, Daniel's thoughts were consumed with Xavier's case, and he couldn't stop thinking about it.

"What's this all about, anyway?" Daniel wondered out loud, his face scrunched up so much only wrinkles showed where his eyes, eyebrows, and forehead should be. Xavier not wanting to take care of another kid? When my boys complain about their complicated female situations, I tell 'em, the world probably wouldn't have to deal with most of these problems if we just handled sex the way God designed it. From what I hear, sex is amazing, and I look forward to having it with Wyni. . . but"

Paul took his eyes off the road long enough to give his son a censorious side eye glare.

"You don't have to worry about me, Dad. All my teenage years I've avoided baby mama drama, paternity tests, child support, STD's or STI's—whatever they are calling them these days. I want no part of that. Even though I've found the one God has for me, I know He will bless me and Wynsome immeasurably for honoring him with our obedience. I know there's gone be fire in the bedroom, the bathroom, the kitchen table. . ." Daniel suddenly realized he had said too much.

Getting serious, Daniel told the older men, "Xavier could be facing double murder, you know, with at least a sentence of life without parole. Miller's dad could face double murder for Michelle's death and the death of that baby girl. And Xavier robbed Miller of the opportunity to grow up with his mother and sister. All children need their mother and father. One senseless act has taken them both away," Daniel lamented.

"What? interrupted Deacon King, I don't mean to cut off ya thought, son, but did I hear ya say double murder -- Michelle and tha baby?"

"Yes sir, I said that," Daniel responded lost in his own thoughts.

"I am ashtoneshid. That is plum crazy," Deacon King said, his booming voice overpowering the small vehicle. "Isn't it legal to have an abortion all over this great nation?"

"Yeah," both Paul and Daniel responded simultaneously. Daniel started unwrapping from his own thoughts to actually focus on Deacon King's words.

"Even up to six months in some states, right?"

"Right," the men said in unison wondering when the Deacon was going to get to the point.

"But if a pregnant woman carrying a child is killed and loses the baby, the killer will be charged with double murder?" Again the men spoke in the affirmative finally catching on.

"Anybody else see the inconsistency here?" this time the men just silently and slowly nodded.

"What if the mama and unborn were killed in a drive-by on her way to the abortion clinic?" Deacon King had a flair for the dramatic. All of them sat in silence deep in thought.

"Ev'body got a different opinion of when life begins. Evidently, life begins when life is wanted. Un-freaking-believable!" Deacon King said, resting his case.

~~~

After another associate ministers' meeting, Rev. Ashley ran to her office to hide before anyone else could pull her aside to complain, gossip, or Lord forbid, whine. She pulled a Buffalo Rock out of her mini fridge and grabbed the bag of gummy bears from her top left drawer. As she tore open the bag with her teeth, she looked down at her cell phone sitting on her desk and saw she had a new email from Jodie. Rev. Ashley was glad to hear from her because they hadn't had a chance to talk in a while.

To: Rev.J.Ashley@church.org
From: J_Sutton@southerntraditionsmail.com
Subject: Catching up

I still can't believe Michelle is gone. I mean we were never friends but our families always hung out together. I just don't know what to think about the whole thing.

Thanks for organizing that volunteer opportunity, even though no one showed up but me! It was a very humbling experience. I showed you the guy I met when you finally got there. He's cute, isn't he? We have been texting back and forth since that day, but we still haven't hung out or even had a phone conversation. People just don't call anymore. All they want to do is text, ugh! I'm in no position to date right now, anyway. I'm trying to get my situation straight with God.

I've been thinking about the things we've been talking about and I realize it's time to make a change. Also, I started creating my own index cards. Thank you for showing me the ones you have done. The process of looking up scriptures that counter the negative thoughts I have about myself is really powerful. You know, I have trouble believing that there is no condemnation in Christ. I just can't shake the feeling that my sins are unforgivable because I knew they were wrong when I did them. But check this out, I found this scripture in 1 John 3:19-20 (NLT):

> Our actions will show that we belong to the truth, so we will be confident when we stand before God. [20] Even if we feel guilty, God is greater than our feelings, and he knows everything.

I ran across this prayer based off of that scripture; I don't remember where I got from. I keep reciting it over and over in my head hoping one day to believe it:

> O God, please set my heart at rest in Your presence when my heart wants to condemn me. For you, God, are greater than my heart, and You know everything.

I wrote this poem recently during one of my deep introspection episodes. Let me know what you think. See you at the next Truthseekers.

CAN'T KEEP RUNNING AWAY

How did I end up in the belly of this fish, again?
My destiny is tied up in God's Will for me
But I keep running, running away.

The words of that Pharcyde song from back in the day
Keeps playing in my mind.
Along with the Bible story about Jonah and the
Ninevites

Jonah's internalized oppression, pride, and strong will
Delayed his obedience to God's direction.

My insecurity, diseased heart, and hurt feelings
Keep me from performing the tasks God sends me.

I just want to be left alone to my own devices,
No more pressure and responsibility
No more community and accountability.

All people seem to do is let me down and harm me.

Running away seems so much easier to do
But I guess they are just as imperfect as I am
Laboring through their own issues.

I can't keep running away-ay-ay.

When I run away I run straight into the belly of the fish.
I wallow in the sea of darkness with mire, gunk and other junk.
I have plenty of time to think about how miserable I am.
The only way out of this state is to allow God to work in me.

I can't KEEP running away.
I can't KEEP running away.

He knows just where to find me.
My free will keeps landing me in obscurity
If I lean on and trust completely in Him
Instead of thinking it's all about me
 Resting in the knowing or knowledge that I am a vessel being used by God
And the buck stops with Him.

It's the God show; I'm just a character in it.
It was on air before my life began and it will be here when my time is up.
I shouldn't waste this part or spend it living in the snow of disconnect.
Just allow God to be in control
And resist the urge to. . .
Keep running away

J Sutton

~~~

Daniel officially moved into Michelle's and Miller's old condo—his condo now. His excitement and nervousness increased when he thought about living by himself and on his own for the first time. Living in the dorm gave him the opportunity to act grown without grown up responsibilities, like bills. He had already started looking for a job so he could cover his utilities and other expenses. Until then his parents would help him out. The thought of his newfound duties made him shudder.

Daniel's college roommates, Brian, Burke, and Ernest, helped him move all his belongings from the dorm and his parents' house to the new spot. Miller was proud of himself for doing his part by carrying the lightweight items.

Finally, the condo was set up the way Daniel envisioned it. He was keeping Michelle's kitchen appliances but that eggplant leather couch she loved so much had to go. He planned to exchange that girly apparatus for a masculine couch as soon as possible.

Tonight, the boys intended to show Miller and Parker the fundamentals of a fantastic guys' night. They planned to stay up late, making a mess of the newly decorated loft, playing video games, horsing around, and eating bad food.

While the festivities were in full swing, Daniel sat back watching the big guys wrestle with the little guys. The big guys let Miller and Parker think they actually had a chance at taking them down. Ernest and Brian, the smallest of the three roommates, eventually pinned Miller down, but Parker went in for a surprise attack, knocking the two guys off of Miller. Basking in his glory, Parker was caught off guard and wrestled to the floor by the big guys; even his best friend Miller turned on him. It was all in fun though.

Daniel's heart swelled as he saw the sheer elation all over Miller's face. He was so relieved that Miller still knew how to just be a kid. While Daniel was deep in thought, Miller blindsided him after he freed Parker from the hold Burke and Ernest had on him. Daniel was flat on the floor with Miller on top of him grinning before he realized he had been knocked down. His old suitemates ragged on him the rest of the night for being ambushed by his little cousin.

Throughout the night, Daniel caught the guys whispering with each other. He felt like they were conspiring against him. Burke texted on his phone for the majority of the night. Around 11:30, the boys suddenly jumped up and announced they were about to leave.

"Why are y'all leaving? I thought we were hanging out all night."

Burke, the group's self-appointed spokesperson, informed Daniel, "We have discussed this among ourselves and have decided it is time for you to become a big boy; therefore, we are leaving so that you can spend your first night in the condo by yourself. Don't thank us. Frankly, we don't know what you would do without us, either. We will even take Miller home and drop Parker off next door for you.

"No, no, no," Parker sang. "This was supposed to be a sleepover. My grandma told me she didn't want to see me again until tomorrow afternoon. I'm going home with Miller," he declared.

"I stand corrected. We will take both Miller and Parker to your parents' house. See you later," Burke stated before they all left in a hurry without another word.

While Daniel was still trying to figure out what just happened, he went into the master bathroom to take a shower. He hadn't realized how tired he was and was kinda relieved they were gone.

Wynsome quietly let herself in using the key Daniel had given her. She placed the grocery bag down on the kitchen counter and searched for him. She was so thankful when she heard the shower running. Her plan has worked out beautifully so far. She had already asked the guys not to stay all night so Daniel could spend his first night in the condo with her.

She returned to the kitchen and started taking out her treats — the bottle of champagne, fresh ripe peaches, pralines, and whipped cream. She thought about freezing cantaloupe slices, too, but decided Daniel wasn't ready for all that yet. Wynsome placed the goodies on one of Michelle's serving trays and set it on the coffee table in front of the eggplant leather couch.

Daniel liked to linger in the shower when he had the time, but Wynsome didn't want him to catch her in the act, so she rushed to pop the bottle of champagne, light the tall candles, queue up the Blu-ray player and remove her outer layer of clothing to reveal a sexy wife-beater top and lacy boy shorts. She turned off the lights, curled up on the couch, and wrapped herself in a thick, warm blanket just as Daniel shut off the shower.

After toweling off and putting on his pajama bottoms, Daniel noticed all the lights were off in the great room, knowing they were on when he left the room. He walked apprehensively into the room to investigate and broke out in a huge grin when he discovered that Wynsome was the perpetrator.

Joining her on the couch, Daniel said seductively, "What are you doing here?"

"I wanted to make your first night in the condo special," she answered, leaning over and kissing him softly.

"So you and the boys set me up and even included my little cousin in your scheme. I thought it was strange when he walked out of here without a fight."

"I plead the fifth," Wynsome replied, holding up five beautifully manicured fingers. She grabbed the Blu-ray case laying on the coffee table. "I brought our favorite movie, Brown Sugar, and prepared some snacks." Putting down the case, Wynsome picked up a peach slice, dipped it in whipped cream, and gave Daniel a taste.

"Are you trying to seduce me?"

"I just want your first night in the condo to be special. Let's toast to many more special days and nights together."

They took a sip of champagne and snuggled up to watch the movie. They stirred only to feed each other peaches dipped in whipped cream topped with pralines. During the awkward scene with Mos Def and Queen

Latifah talking in the kitchen, Wynsome placed her head on Daniel's bare chest where her hand had been resting. A few seconds later, she took Daniel's left hand and placed it on her left thigh at the point in the movie when Mos Def clumsily tried to explain to Queen Latifah that champagne flutes were designed to emulate the seductive shape of a woman.

Taking advantage of the shock on Daniel's face, Wynsome gave him a passionate, extended kiss. Not wanting to break from their kiss, Wynsome stood to her feet and gave Daniel a wonderful look at her in her lingerie. Pulling him in a standing position, she led him to the bedroom but once there, Daniel took the lead.

He laid Wynsome down the length of the bed and climbed on top of her and ravenously peeled off her lacy boy shorts and camisole. Sitting up on his knees, Daniel stopped to admire her full gorgeousness. Wynsome playfully licked Daniel's neck, lessening his resolve. At his most vulnerable spot, Wynsome took back control. With her on top, she stripped off the Joe Boxer pajama bottoms she had bought him and reached for the condom she had asked Burke to hide under his pillow. While giving her full attention to his nipples, she expertly slipped the condom on him.

Even though his body was telling a different story, Daniel wasn't as excited as he thought he would be at this moment. He couldn't shake the uneasiness at how well Wynsome maneuvered that condom. Daniel knew she wasn't a virgin, but dang! And how did the condom get under his pillow anyway?

Daniel knew they needed to stop but figured they may have already gone too far to turn back now.

As Wynsome nibbled on his earlobe while rubbing one of his nipples between her thumb and index finger, Daniel abruptly ended the four play. He sat up with her still on top of him; straddling him. He pulled her into a long-drawn-out bear hug then repositioned her on the bed next to him.

"You need to go."

Bewildered, Wynsome said, "What?!" No man had ever told her no or stop or anything like that.

"Wynsome, I love you, but you must put your clothes on and leave."

Breathing deeply, "I'm really tired of going through this with you, Daniel; getting me all worked up and then stopping. What kind of game are you playing?" Only silence came from Daniel.

"Trying a different approach, "And you know you don't like for me to drive late at night," Wynsome said almost pleading.

That gave Daniel pause, but he decided to stick to his decision, "No, I don't. But, it is the best thing for you to do. Leave. Now."

Wynsome picked up her underwear and went into the living room to redress. She moved slowly, hoping Daniel would come in, apologize, and take her back to his bed but he never did. Defeated and angry, Wynsome left the condo, closing the door softly.

||||| |||||

As Jodie took her seat on the airplane, she looked at her cell one more time before take-off. The same two text messages were still there, one from Rev. Ashley checking to see if she still planned to come to Truthseekers that evening and the other from Amir. Jodie's shoulders tensed as she read the text from him-

> I won't be able to meet you at the airport.
> Take the shuttle to the hotel.
> Don't wait on me to eat and have it tight for me when I get there.

Jodie powered off her cell and locked her seatbelt in place. She tried to shake off the nagging feeling building within her spirit. She knew going to see Amir was a bad idea, but it was too late to back out now. She had just renewed her commitment to God, too. She admitted to herself this decision could lead her back down the wrong road. Jodie shook it off, convincing herself she was overreacting. She tried to relax and prepared to have an amazing time in New York. Settling in her aisle seat, she opened up a book, *A Piece of Cake,* by Cupcake Brown. She had bought it at the gift shop in the Birmingham airport.

Jodie had been so engrossed in her book she was taken aback when the captain announced they were about to land. When the plane landed, she stood patiently waiting on the passenger in front of her. His behind was stuck in the air as he fumbled around under his seat looking for something. She was finally able to tread into the large airport. Trembling, her body betrayed her as she walked in and looked around for signs directing her to the baggage area. She found it and quickly pulled her luggage off the conveyor belt.

As soon as Jodie walked into the New York airport, a man ran up to her and grabbed her bags.

"Ma'am, I can take you to your hotel in my limousine for a thirty-dollar flat rate." Excitedly, Jodie agreed but her heart sank when his limo appeared in sight. It was beat up, dented, dusty, and old.

"Um, sir, I think I'll pass. I don't feel comfortable riding in that." Surprisingly, he didn't put up a fight and readily gave back her luggage. Jodie hurriedly found a cab with a friendly driver to take her to her hotel, arriving around 3:30.

As soon as Jodie entered the plush hotel room, she unpacked and texted Amir to let him know she had arrived safely. He had already told her he didn't get off work until 5:00p.m. He responded back with more frustrating news:

> My car is making a weird noise so I'm going to stop at a car repair shop real quick to get it checked out.

Jodie fought the urge to get upset. Giving him the benefit of the doubt, she decided to believe him and head down to the hotel's restaurant for dinner. Jodie wasn't accustomed to traveling in big cities alone and would not dare step outside the hotel by herself unless it was to the airport. The restaurant was practically empty;

maybe because it was extremely expensive. She ordered the grilled shrimp with pasta and a glass of red wine, hoping for a calming effect and a more jovial mode. Jodie called Emberli from her cell to keep her company.

"Hey, girl. Why didn't you make it to work today? You know you are supposed to give me a heads up when you are going to play hooky," Emberli said as soon as she picked up the phone.

"I didn't want you to try to talk me out of it."

"What have you done? Where are you?"

"In New York," Jodie answered matter-of-factly.

"You know what, girl, I can't even trip. I got problems of my own."

"What?! I know this is serious if you aren't trying to get all up in my business. Everything alright with you and Nate?"

"Girl, I don't know. I'll tell you more about that when you get home. I guess you aren't going to make it to Truthseekers tonight. I was just getting ready to go. I need some Jesus right about now."

"Don't we both," Jodie said to Emberli before they wrapped up their conversation.

After dinner, Jodie went back to her hotel room. By now, it was the seven o'clock hour, and Amir should arrive soon, so she pulled out her negligee and took a shower to prepare for his arrival. After showering and beautifying, she began reading the book she bought in the airport to keep her occupied. She was so absorbed in the book during the flight, she couldn't wait to finish it. As soon as she opened the book, her cell phone buzzed again.

I'm stuck in traffic.
I'm trying to get there as soon as possible.

The time was now 9:00 p.m. and Jodie was officially PO'd. She slammed the book down, put on her jeans and black fitted shirt over her negligee and went down to the hotel's bar. Surprisingly, the bar didn't have many customers in it, either, just like the restaurant. Jodie sat at the bar and ordered a Long Island Iced Tea, getting angrier as she sat there thinking about all the sacrifices she had made to come to New York to see Amir. She spent money she didn't have and even made arrangements to make the trip extra special. Tomorrow they were scheduled for a couple's massage in the privacy of their hotel room.

Jodie took one sip of her drink. *They don't water down their drinks in New York; this is thoroughly strong.* She finished it in three long gulps. When she stood to head back to her hotel room, her legs were a little shaky from the effects of the drink. She quickly regained her balance and headed out the bar. She missed a step down exiting the bar and entering the hotel lobby area, falling flat on her face and landing sprawled out on the carpet as if posing for a chalk outline at a crime scene. Her elbow broke her fall slightly and stung profusely. Jodie was so glad she had not worn the five-inch freak 'em heels she had brought specifically for Amir's pleasure. It would be horrible to have broken a bone and be lying up in a New York hospital right now.

Several older Jewish ladies seated in the hotel lobby came over and asked if she needed any help. Jodie waved them all away, insisting she could handle getting

150

up on her own. Embarrassed, Jodie walked back to the room with a sore knee, elbow, and pride. As she disrobed her first layer of clothing, she discovered a huge carpet burn below her right elbow.

Frustrated, Jodie texted Amir and told him she was going to bed without him. He immediately responded saying he was almost there. It was now 10:45, and Jodie was beyond pissed.

Soon after, she heard a knock on the door but waited several minutes before answering. She eventually opened the door with rage written all over her face.

"You didn't hear me knocking?" Amir said, matching her facial expression with just as much arrogance.

"Yeah," Jodie responded with a 'what's your point' tone of voice.

Leaning over to give her a hug, Amir said, "Girl, how long has it been since we've seen each other? I've missed you." He thought the elapsed time between visits excused his lack of respect, as if she should just be happy to see him.

Jodie lay down in the bed as he took off his bucket hat, shirt, and shoes, and then lay down next to her. Without delay, he started massaging her shoulders, but Jodie was not in the mood and his inconsiderate aggressiveness was making her angrier. She had made all these sacrifices for him, but his selfish ways still prevailed. Breathing deeply, she reminded herself she promised to be on her best behavior. She neglected to tell him that her best behavior was contingent on whether or not he stayed on his.

Calming down, she laid on his chest savoring his smell. She had forgotten how good it felt to be close to him. He slightly tugged on her hair while tilting her head up until her lips met his. Soon they were caught in the throngs of intercourse. After it was all over, Jodie still felt unsatisfied and empty inside. Having sex with Amir had not brought the joy she thought it would, and she realized she went back on her commitment to God for something that wasn't worth it, which made her feel worse about herself. All of these thoughts caused her to sob uncontrollably. Amir didn't know what to do or think. This was a first for him. He couldn't fathom what could have made her cry.

Amir asked the obvious, "Are you crying?"

"No," Jodie replied as her sobs got louder and louder. Abruptly, she got up and ran into the bathroom hoping to get herself together. She looked herself in the mirror and all she saw was defeat. *What am I doing here? Why am I still wasting my time with this man? What's wrong with me?* God kept providing a way of escape for her when the circumstances seemed impossible, but she kept going back to the wrong thing.

God had spared her from disease and pregnancy. They did have a pregnancy scare once when the condom had come off in the middle of sex, but Jodie had bought a dose of Plan B immediately, what some call the abortion pill. She didn't know if it was or if it wasn't, she just didn't want to be pregnant and especially not by this man. These thoughts made her feel even worse about herself, activating a waterfall of tears down her face. Eventually, she got it together enough to return back to bed.

Amir and Jodie both lay on their backs with their shoulders two inches apart, just staring at the ceiling. Both of them deep in thought, there was silence between them for several moments.

Into the tense air, Amir finally asked, "Why were you crying? What's the problem? What have you done?"

What does he mean, 'what have I done?'

"Are you cheating? Do you have a man back home?" he asked.

She knew her actions must have come off really strange. She couldn't think of the right words to explain to Amir exactly how she was feeling and she really didn't have the energy to try. He wouldn't understand or care anyway. She was just tired of making the same mistakes over and over again. Jodie felt there was no hope for her.

"I'm just fed up. There are so many things wrong with this situation. This casual sexual relationship isn't working for me. It hurts because I feel like I'm just your jump-off. Do you realize how disrespectful it was for you to have me waiting for so long when I flew thousands of miles and spent money I didn't have to come see you! I'm mad at myself, ok. I'm mad at you, too. You are beyond selfish."

They both lay there in silence again for several minutes before Amir leaned over and tried to comfort Jodie. Even though she was mad, she had sex with him again, hoping the empty feeling would go away and she would instead feel the connection they used to have. As the night grew long, they ended up falling asleep holding hands only to wake in the middle of the night to go at it again.

Jodie still felt empty but was hopeful the weekend would get better until Amir flipped the script on her again. He told her he had to go to work for a few hours but he would not be gone for long. Jodie resisted the temptation to get pissed and tried to stay positive as they fell back asleep.

In the morning, Amir got up, took a shower and got ready to go to work. He tried to sneak out of the hotel room without telling Jodie goodbye.

"You're not going to say anything?" Jodie asked.

"I didn't want to wake you. I'm going to work."

"Okay." Then he walked out of the door. That was the last time she saw him on that trip.

By late morning, Jodie got up to take a shower. After getting dressed, she went to the hotel's restaurant for breakfast, and then took her good book to the poolside. Around 3:30, she went back to the room to prepare for their couple's massage. As she inserted the card key in the reader, she heard her cell phone buzz from inside. She was excited to see it was a message from Amir.

> I got a job offer to work on a music video shoot today. I really need to take it because I need the money.

"What the f***," Jodie yelled at the top of her lungs. "I did not come all the way from Alabama to be stood up." She dialed Amir's cell number over and over until he finally picked up.

"You don't have the decency to call me and tell me this BS. You have to tell me through a freaking text message?" Jodie yelled through the phone.

"Hey, I was on the phone with the executives from the video shoot and was going to call you when I finished talking to them."

"Really, Amir? Are you really doing this to me?"

"Hey, I can turn the job down if you give me the two hundred dollars I would make on the video shoot." Jodie began cursing, screaming, and crying.

"All that crying you did last night helped me make this decision. I don't want to be around a sad and depressed person. I'm in a bad place right now myself, and I don't need any more sadness around me."

"Will I see you again before I leave tomorrow?"

"Do you know how far away from you I am? No, I need to conserve my gas."

"I'm far away from home too. I came all the way from Birmingham, AL to see you," Jodie said wailing.

"I'm going to have to hang up this phone if you keep up that crying." She cried louder and he kept his word for a change and hung up.

Jodie threw her cell phone against the wall. She sobered up real fast though because she needed that phone to get back home. She picked it up and put it back together to call him back. Thank God, it still worked.

"You owe me the cost of this trip, and you will pay me back for my expenses," Jodie said and hung up.

She went to the gift shop and bought some Tylenol PM. The only way she was going to get through this horrible situation was to sleep, and she could only sleep with the help of a sleep aid. She went back to the room, took the pills, and called Patrick from church. She hadn't talked to him in a long time, but she needed him. He did a good job of making her feel good about herself. He really knew how to gas her up. They managed to have a fun, light-hearted conversation that helped her to feel much better. She told him she would connect with him when she got back in town.

The rest of the trip was a blur. When she checked out of the hotel, her bill had charges she did not make. Apparently, Amir had helped himself to the food in the mini-fridge without her knowledge or consent. He had the audacity to charge his parking to her room as well. She texted him immediately with his total and her address so he could mail his re-imbursement. He should have a little bit of money now from that video shoot. Of course, she knew she would never receive it. Hopefully, she would never see him again, either.

⊬⊬⊬ ⊬⊬⊬ Ⅰ

Rev. Ashley sat in the young adult Bible study class praying passionately before Truthseekers began. She was so frustrated with these young people God entrusted her with that she wanted to use bad words, such bad words. They had been inconsistent with their church duties, missing worship services, and avoiding her attempts to get in touch with them. Only Emberli and Patrick had shown up at their last meeting. Rev. Ashley knew from first-hand experience that was never a good sign. Trying to keep it holy, she prayed for the Lord to sanctify her tongue and the Holy Spirit to lead her to say the right words that would touch them in the way they needed it most.

As they trickled in the room, all of the young people avoided making eye contact with Rev. Ashley.

"I'm so glad to see you all tonight. It has been quite a while since all of us have been here. Go ahead and help yourself to the refreshments. We will talk as we eat." The young people silently fixed their plates while Rev. Ashley removed empty seats from the semi-circle to keep the group as intimate as possible.

When her new friend Wade walked through the door, only then did Jodie remember inviting him. She didn't recognize him at first and couldn't believe he actually showed up. They had only communicated through text and email since meeting at the Homeless Connect event.

As Jodie stood in line at the snack table, Wade walked up to her with a single yellow rose and a small yellow stuffed bunny in his arms. When he handed her the present, they embraced in a sideways church-lady hug. All the other young adults tried not to stare. No one had ever seen Jodie with a guy before. She always seemed so standoffish.

"You didn't have to come with gifts," Jodie said as she grinned, cradling the bear in the bend of her left arm.

"I thought I shouldn't come empty-handed since I haven't seen you in so long. You look beautiful," Wade said with a smile, examining her from her natural hair to the top-siders on her feet. Jodie returned his warm greeting. Her cheeks blossomed into a rose tint. There her body went, betraying her again. Blushing was hard for her to do with her flawless dark skin.

As everyone settled down in their seats with refreshments, Rev. Ashley opened in prayer and went over the norms before starting the discussion.

"I haven't had a chance for an in-depth conversation with most of you since we lost two of our members. What are your thoughts regarding Michelle's death and Xavier's imprisonment?" I know it had an effect on each of you, even if you didn't have a close relationship with either one.

"You told me that you were positive that Michelle would come out of this victoriously. She didn't. How do you explain that?" Wynsome said at full volume. She surprised herself with the spontaneous outburst.

Sitting on top of a chair with her feet in the seat and her elbows on her knees, Rev. Ashley responded tenderly, "She did come out victorious. She is in a much better place now and God used her death to bring many people to Christ. We will never know the full impact of how things turned out."

"So you are saying it was God's will to leave Miller without his mother *and* father?" Jodie said with her arms folded, insolent.

"Yes," Rev. Ashley simply said.

"That's some bull right there. What kind of God does that?" asked Emberli before sucking her teeth.

"We forget that when we accepted Christ, we accepted him as Savior *and* Lord. We love how He saves us from our sins but we conveniently forget that He is also Lord. He is sovereign, self-governing. He gets to do what He wants to do when He wants to do it and how He wants to do it. He may not let us in on the ways He chooses to operate. The sooner we surrender to that, the easier life will be."

"Humph. . .that's your opinion," Emberli replied.

"No, that's a fact. Not my opinion."

Jodie said, "How can you be so sure?" but added sarcastically, "I know, I know. The Holy Spirit revealed it to you." *She speaks with such self-assurance, and that annoys the hell out of me!* Jodie thought to herself.

"Yes, and He will reveal it to you, too, through His Word. While everyone continued to avoid eye contact with Rev. Ashley, Wade thought it best to stay silent himself since he didn't know anything about what they were talking about. He felt like he had walked into a hostile family reunion, instead of a Bible study.

Breaking his silence, Daniel said with his shoulders slumped over, "I've tried reading the Word, but I just don't feel like it." "I'm at the point now where

I just want to not be bothered and just watch Pastor Longhorn online.

"Daniel, you have been through some tough stuff. There are many changes going on in your life on top of your grief. Your feelings are completely valid and understandable, but don't stay down too long or isolate yourself. Satan wants to devour you and render you useless. I know God has a wonderful call on all of your lives."

Sitting straight up on the edge of her chair, fully engaged for a change, Jodie said to Rev. Ashley, "I really admire your relationship with the Lord and all. And your ability to remind yourself on the regular that this life isn't about you but it's about God. But at the same time, I feel like you have unrealistic expectations. Times have changed."

"Yeah! You are being pushy, almost to the point of bullying. Shoot, got me mad all up in the church!" Emberli admonished, swirling her right index finger into figure eights.

"These are not my expectations," Rev. Ashley said. "These are God's. I only shared what the Holy Spirit told me to share. Y'all need to quit with all these justifications! For real, for real. There aren't nearly enough crutches in the world for all these lame excuses. Pick up your mat and walk, young people! Y'all should be at a deeper level in your relationship with God at this point and more concerned about pleasing Him."

Nodding his head, Daniel sighed. "We can't say we don't know the right things to do, Rev. Ashley, but sometimes it gets hard. Especially when you do things the right way and the right way isn't getting you the results you were looking for.

"Focus less on results and more on fruit," Rev. Ashley stated.

Without thinking about it, Emberli yelled, "What the f*** does that mean?"Gurrrrl," Jodie said giving Emberli an evil sideways glance before she could even finish her inappropriate statement. Nothing else had to be said.

"I thought they were one and the same," Jodie said to Rev. Ashley with a perplexed look after setting Emberli straight.

"Sometimes God is shifting, molding us into his image; that is the fruit he is looking for. He is more concerned about that than you getting that relationship you asked for or preventing the death of a loved one you prayed so hard about. It's all about relationship, young people," Rev. Ashley concluded.

~~~

Jodie and Wade sat in the empty Sunday school class. They sat at the rectangular table in the very back of the room; each of them took a seat on the opposite side of the table that separated them. The room appeared very dark and hollow with just the two of them in it, probably because of the blinking fluorescent lights. Everyone else had quickly left after the meeting ended.

"I'm so sorry the conversation was so touchy and heavy tonight. I didn't expect that to happen," Jodie said.

"No need to apologize. I wanted to see you again, anyway. I'm interested in getting to know you better."

Jodie cleared her throat before she responded, her voice deeper than usual, "Hold up. I want you to know exactly what kind of girl you are dealing with here. My relationship with God is very important to me. I am not interested in casual dating; actually not in any kind of dating right now."

"Whoa. I'm not suggesting we leave here and fly to Cabo tonight. Unless you have a passport? Kidding, kidding," he said with a grin. "I was thinking more like jazz in the park this weekend. We can make it more of a group thing and you can invite the rest of your friends. I'd like for all of us to be friends." Wade assured her.

"What friends?" Jodie asked. "I don't have any friends."

"I thought that everyone in Truthseekers were close friends."

"We just attend church together. I don't trust people easily, so I usually just stick to myself. Now, me and Emberli are friends. Our friendship works because we don't expect or even want each other to get too deep or personal."

"Okay, you don't date and you don't have any friends. Sounds like an isolated life. What do you do?" Wade inquired.

"I told you, I'm working on my relationship with God."

"That's cool. I actually hadn't dated in a long time myself. I can't really say it was intentional, though," Wade answered honestly. "This is probably too much information too soon but I can be very judgmental."

Jodie found it refreshing that Wade talked so candidly about himself and his flaws.

Oh really. "In what way?" Jodie asked.

"I get easily annoyed when people don't do things the way I think they should be done. You know, because what Wade says is always best," he joked.

"Honesty, I like that. I'm glad you recognize that about yourself."

"Thank you, it means a lot to hear you say that. A guy can get a little insecure when he allows himself to be vulnerable in front of a beautiful lady."

Rolling her eyes and crossing her arms, Jodie warned, "Please don't ruin a great conversation with gratuitous flirting."

"I didn't mean any harm by it, Miss Lady. You can uncross those arms of yours. But yeah, I now understand that the same grace God extends to me is the same grace I should extend to everyone else. After I actually started putting that into practice, my relationship with God has grown so much."

Jodie noticed through her peripheral vision that Deacon Rouser was peeping into the room. When he realized he had been caught, he opened the door and asked if they had seen his daughter. Jodie told him Rev. Ashley had left over a half hour ago. Disappointed, he told them they had to end their courting session now because he was about to lock the church up.

Jodie and Wade reluctantly ended their conversation. When Wade started to escort Jodie out of the building, Deacon Rouser followed close on their heels. The Deacon rudely locked the church doors without even a goodbye as soon as they stepped outside.

Such a gentleman, Wade followed Jodie to her car and opened her car door for her. She watched him in her rearview mirror as he made sure she made it out of the dark parking lot safely. Jodie felt like a schoolgirl with a crush and wished she had someone she could call to share her joy with. *Maybe I do need some friends,* Jodie thought to herself.

~~~

Jodie sat at her computer, attempting to compose an email to Rev. Ashley. She was frustrated because she couldn't seem to find the right words to describe how she was feeling. She felt convicted to fess up to her trip to New York. This conversation was probably best to have in person. Jodie didn't want Rev. Ashley to misunderstand what she was trying to get across.

Jodie pressed past her comfort zone and called Rev. Ashley. She reasoned it was just as good as talking in person.

When Rev. Ashley answered, Jodie jumped right in. "Rev. Ashley, we need to talk."

"Well hi, Jodie. Please forgive me for breathing heavy into the phone. I just finished exercising. They say it's good for improving your mental clarity. I could use some more of that right about now. Give me a chance to catch my breath. "

"Oh, I can call you back a little later."

"No, no. That is not necessary. What's on your mind?" Rev. Ashley said as she stopped the treadmill, grabbed her bottle of water and plopped down on the couch in her workout room/office.

Straying from her computer chair to her California Queen-sized bed, Jodie blurted out the whole story about visiting Amir in New York and the disaster it turned out to be. She rambled on about how much she hated herself and how horrible her witness for Christ must be.

"I'm beginning to realize I compromised myself greatly by staying involved with Amir. As a woman of God, I should expect so much more out of the men I spend time with. I shouldn't be wasting my good years with guys like him," Jodie continued.

"Jodie, you must learn not to be so hard on yourself. Now yes, God has provided many ways of escape for you. You say you want to be in a committed, loving relationship, but you aren't allowing room in your life for God to move. He can't send you the right thing if you are continuing to entertain the wrong thing."

With a faint crackle, Jodie said "Remember the nickname you gave Amir—Splenda? I giggle every time I think of it. But seriously, Rev. Ashley, tell me exactly what I need to do."

"I think you have become too dependent on me when you should be depending on Christ for these answers. That is my fault. I take full responsibility for that. Lord, forgive me," Rev. Ashley said taking a swig of water and grabbing the bag of gummy bears off the sofa table.

There was a long silence between them before finally, Rev. Ashley inquired, "Are you okay?"

"Yeah. I'm just deep in thought."

"Well, I'll let you go. Don't think too deeply on your own. You may get it wrong. Pray!" Rev. Ashley hung up the phone without saying goodbye.

Jodie laid flat on her stomach straight across her bed with her head hanging off the side. She lay there and poured her heart out to God. After what seemed like hours, Jodie began to feel God moving in her spirit. She got up immediately and started writing in her journal the words that suddenly flooded her brain. She couldn't get the words down on the paper fast enough.

My love is complete and it will never change. I will never give up on you. Is that not enough for you, my child? Your worth is in me. You don't have to work for my approval because you are already forgiven, you are loved unconditionally. Stop striving, stop trying to prove yourself. Know that as my child, as my daughter, you deserve much better than what you have been settling for. Not because of anything you have done but because I love my children and I treat my children well. Why have you been giving my pearls to swine? Believe in me. Love me. Obey me. Wait on me. I will not be moved by your temper tantrums. When doubt arises, remind yourself that your daddy has this all under control. Chill out.

"*Wow! I have never heard from the Lord that clearly before!*" Jodie said to herself as she continued to write. A wave of peace washed over her, and she knew in her spirit God had delivered her from the low self-esteem that had led her to accept less than she deserved. She sat there worshiping, praising, and thanking God for being God. Jodie repented for not trusting Him and for not believing in Him.

Looking up to the heavens, Jodie prayed aloud, "I have allowed myself to get so wrapped up in myself and so focused on the things of this world, that I lost sight of who You are. I'm sorry for allowing the quest for love and affection and the pursuit of acceptance to become my gods."

~~~

By the time Wade showed up at Jodie's door, she was ready to go and have a good time. They planned to see Savion Glover at the University Theater. It was Wade's idea. Jodie had never considered going to see a grown man tap dance on stage by himself. Surprisingly both of them enjoyed the show and were disappointed they had to leave early to make their dinner reservations at the swanky new restaurant in Alabaster. The restaurant was Wade's idea, too. Jodie much rather preferred to go to the fish and rib joint in Ensley. She didn't mind that you couldn't see the cooks through the cutout window in the wall; all you could see was the same greasy hand taking your order handing you your food.

At the end of the night, Jodie had conflicting emotions. She never wanted the night to end when she was in Wade's company. When Wade pulled up in her driveway after they left the restaurant, she didn't want the night to be over so she invited him in for a cup of coffee, and he happily accepted.

Wade admired her immaculately decorated home. Jodie lived in a garden home with vaulted ceilings, a huge kitchen and a screened-in back porch. Her home was adorned with soft pastels of yellow, pink, and heather grey. Somehow, it worked without looking like an Easter basket.

Jodie led him from the living room through the kitchen to the back porch, which was complete with a flat screen television and surround sound system. Jodie turned on the television as they made themselves comfortable on the plush grey couch. The TV was already tuned to ESPN2. Wade couldn't believe Jodie was a sports fan. This girl was too good to be true. They snuggled on the couch, laughing and talking while watching tennis highlights until they both dozed off to sleep.

‖‖‖ ‖‖‖ ‖‖

On a rainy Thursday morning in late August, Carol and Paul sat side-by-side on a bench in Judge Cavern's small courtroom. They were nervously waiting for Xavier's sentencing hearing to start.

Judge Cavern didn't look anything like Carol had envisioned. He just didn't look like a judge with his pale skin and frail frame. His hair was cut into an early-career Justin Beiber style but flaming red! A short man, he only stood about 5 feet 4 inches and had a deep baritone voice.

Daniel sat next to Michelle's father, Bernard on the third row. Rev. Ashley and Pastor Longhorn sat on the bench behind where the Roberts sat on the second row. Xavier's distraught mother was the sole person sitting on the opposite side of the courtroom. Cheryl refused to come and refused to allow their children to see their dad in that condition. She didn't even let them visit him in jail. Ever since their divorce, Xavier has felt like Cheryl wanted to punish him. For what, he didn't know. He did know she wanted the divorce just as much as he did, even though it was hard for both of them to accept that their forever actually had an expiration date.

The judge had done Xavier a favor by expediting his case. Xavier pled no contest to the double murder charges for the murder of Michelle and their baby girl. Those charges carried a maximum sentence of the death penalty, but due to no prior criminal record, his exemplary service on the University's police force, and the favorable testimonies of the Roberts and Bernard, his charges were reduced to involuntary manslaughter.

The judge sentenced Xavier to life in prison with the possibility of parole.

Before leaving the courtroom, Xavier turned to face Michelle's family to apologize one last time.

"I'm earnestly sorry for accidentally ending Michelle's life and causing you so much pain. I am suffering just as much as you are. I loved her. Miller loved her, and I'm being sent away for a long time without ready access to my kids. I promise to maintain so I can get out as soon as possible to be a good father to my sons and daughter."

He then turned to his mother with loving and pleading eyes but choked up when he tried to speak. The bailiff approached Xavier from the side and ushered him out of the courtroom, preventing him from trying to comfort his mother. Secretly, Xavier was relieved. He didn't know what to say that would ease his mother's sorrow.

After the judge and attorneys left the room, the Roberts tried to comfort Xavier's mom. They had all been family for the last seven or so years, and that love hadn't dissipated. Pastor Longhorn insisted they all pray together and ask for God's protection and direction for all of them.

After Pastor Longhorn finally finished his prayer, Daniel looked down at his phone to find a text from Wynsome. She had moved back home over the summer break, so she asked him to come over to her parents' house to hang out and relax after an extremely draining day in court. He didn't have the energy to be good company right now because he was emotionally spent. His text back to her asked for a rain check. Before the night was over, he had promised to come over soon for dinner with her family.

~~~

It was eerily quiet when Daniel walked in his childhood home. He found Miller asleep on the couch. Daniel hadn't been to his parents' house in a while; they had met at the courthouse the last time they saw each other. He was long overdue for a visit.

The floorboard squealed under his feet as he looked for at least one of his parents. Surely, they wouldn't leave the kid by himself. His mom was nowhere to be found, but he stumbled upon his father standing in the kitchen, drinking a cup of tea while staring out the back window.

"Dad, why is it so quiet in here?" Daniel asked, walking right up behind his father.

"Give me a little space, son," Paul said, pushing his son back. "This is a rare occasion since Miller has been living here. Believe me, I am savoring every minute of the quiet. Your mom went shopping with Oneilia."

Making sure his dad had enough personal space, Daniel said, "Oh, I'm sorry for startling you. I'll be much more careful next time; don't want any accidents to happen. Do you remember when Michelle was living here and it was her turn to wash the dishes? I would jump up outside that window while it was completely dark outside and scare her every time. That never got old," Daniel reminisced.

With a deep chuckle, Paul replied, "Yeah, I remember that. She got .38 hot every time, but for some reason she never anticipated it happening again. You always caught her off guard."

"I'm so glad you came by, son. I need to spend more quality time with my precious son," Paul said, patting Daniel on the back before taking a seat at the breakfast nook.

"Uh oh . . . am I in trouble?" Daniel asked as he took a seat next to his father.

"No, no son. I just want to catch up with you. How do you like living in the condo by yourself?"

Playing with the colorful pickled vegetable centerpiece on the breakfast nook, Daniel answered, "It was weird at first, but I've gotten used to it and I love it now."

"Great. How is Wynsome? You should bring her by sometime to visit with your mother. And you know Miller loves hanging out with her, too."

"Actually Dad, I think me and Wynsome need to have a serious talk. We aren't on the same page about some things."

"Is that right? Does it have anything to do with Wynsome leaving your condo at, umm, an 'ungodly hour'? At least that's how Hazel described it. "

"Ms. Jamison . . . I forgot about her," Daniel mumbled.

"Yeah, your neighbor and your cousin's best friend's grandmother, not to mention the mouth of the South," Paul reiterated and emphasized.

"Yeah, that night is what I need to talk to Wynsome about. I thought we were both committed to not having sex before we got married. We've had a few close calls before, but we have never gotten as far as we did that night. Brian did try to warn me her convictions were not as strong as mine, but I didn't want to believe him."

"Son, you can't put all the blame on Wynsome. I'm sure you were a willing participant, and if you and Wynsome are going to be married one day, you will be the spiritual head of the household, Daniel."

"Yeah, Dad, but it seems Wynsome has a lot of experi. . ."

"Society wants to put the responsibility on the female because 'boys will be boys.' Let me tell you, no offspring of mine will operate like that," Paul interrupted. "The Roberts respect women and treat them honorably. You should not have allowed it to get to that point."

"You're right."

"Now, I'm glad that you did stop. It's not too late to straighten up. Do not use this as an excuse to 'go ahead and do it anyway because you've already gone too far.' That's a lie from the pits of hell. Pray, son, and then have a sit down with Wynsome."

Carol walked in in time to witness her son giving his father a pound on the back as if they were fraternity brothers. She greeted her husband with a kiss, hugged Daniel, and walked out of the room with her words lingering behind, "I'm glad y'all love each other so much and all that, but Paul, I hope you have set your son straight. Don't make me have to do it." Both Roberts' men said in unison, "Yes, ma'am.

Wade worshiped with Jodie at Church at least twice a month all summer long. They continued talking on the phone, texting, and emailing each other constantly—sometimes late into the night 'til early morning—but things still felt awkward between the two of them whenever they were in each other's presence.

During their last conversation, Jodie invited Wade out to lunch at one of her favorite restaurants on the Southside. She needed the Lord's help to keep her emotions in check. Jodie got the warm and fuzzies every time she thought of him; she often had to stop herself from daydreaming about him. They needed to have a conversation soon to set some guidelines before things got out of control.

Wade was the first to arrive at the restaurant and stood in front of the place in the hot September sun until she pulled up. Before they entered through the large wooden door, Wade kissed her on the cheek, causing her to swoon. He had to know the effect he had on her. Jodie was afraid she had fallen hard for this guy.

They were seated in the front window of the restaurant where they could see all the passers-by. As soon as they were settled in their seats, Wade started talking a mile a minute, as if he was trying to overcompensate for his nervousness.

"I was pleasantly surprised to get an invitation to lunch. I've wanted to spend more alone time with you," Wade admitted.

"I'm glad you accepted. I've wanted to spend more time with you, too. That's why I asked you to lunch," Jodie answered coyly.

"Really?" Wade said.

"I don't know if-if you can tell . . . but. . . I am very attracted to you," Jodie replied, stammering. Her mother always taught her never to run behind a man, but patience was not a virtue Jodie had mastered yet.

She bravely continued, "Physically and intellectually." She paused hoping he would validate her with his affection as well. Filling in the silence, she went on, "I must admit, I could easily fall for you." *I should not have admitted that.*

"I'm with you," Wade simply responded.

"What exactly does that mean, 'I'm with you'?" Jodie inquired.

Wade chuckled slightly which transformed into a loud belch, "Oh, excuse me. That's embarrassing. I feel the exact same way," he said with a huge grin on his face.

Jodie tried hard to contain her joy. "I'm glad to hear that," she added simply.

Wade abruptly picked up the menu and asked Jodie what she would recommend for lunch. Confused, Jodie tried to go with the flow.

"I think you would like the beef and broccoli. I'm just going to get an order of the crispy squid myself."

"Crispy squid?" Wade asked skeptically.

"Yeah, calamari," Jodie clarified. She knew from their many chats that he did not like to try new foods. "If you are not too scared, you should try some. I promise you will love it!"

"That's okay. I'm good," Wade answered definitively.

After they placed their orders, the table was covered in silence. Neither of them wanted the burden of maintaining the conversation. Jodie didn't understand why this was so difficult for them when they talked on the phone almost every day. Wade seemed content just watching the people go in and out of the coffee house across the street.

Jodie was determined to have this conversation with Wade today, so she started again, "So. . . I think it's important for us to set some boundaries. You know, we have been talking a lot lately."

"Has that been a problem? You just confirmed that you enjoyed our long talks."

"I do, but I'm not trying to get caught up, you feel me?"

Now Wade was the one confused. He thought they had just agreed that they wanted to explore the caught-up feeling, but he must have interpreted her words incorrectly, so he just played it cool. "I really admire your commitment to doing things God's way," Wade said "I respect that. So what are we going to do differently?"

"First, limit our emails to once a day, but not during work hours. And I don't think we should talk on the phone more than twice a week and only before nine."

"I see you have given this some serious thought. Those are some steep rules. Is all that necessary? I mean, it's doable. I don't want to do it, but I will if you really think it's necessary."

"Oh, it's necessary. I've gotten my feelings entangled then hurt enough times to know it's definitely necessary."

"I'm willing to sacrifice our time together for a greater reward in the end," Wade said to Jodie but he thought to himself, *this girl is wild. She know ain't no grown man going along with that. She won't even be able to go along with that!*

~~~

Jodie signed on to her computer at work and opened her page on the latest, hottest social networking site. She knew she shouldn't be checking it at work, but she just wanted to post a comment really quick.

I am learning I am much stronger than I give myself credit for.

She noticed Rev. Ashley was online as well and sent her an instant message.

> *jsutton*: Shouldn't you be tarrying with the Lord? Aren't you preaching on Sunday?

> *jashley:* Yes. Don't go telling other people though. You know church people don't show up when they know Pastor isn't preaching.

Does Southern Traditions pay you to make posts, while you are trying to call me out?

jsutton: I won't tell nobody. And I stand corrected.

jashley: So, what is the story behind your post because I know there has to be a story?

jsutton: I was just thinking that I've learned a lot about myself since I met Wade.

jashley: Do tell.

Jodie looked over her shoulder and repositioned her vanity mirror so she could see who walked behind her. She didn't want to get caught goofing off by her new overly zealous supervisor. When the coast was clear, Jodie resumed her conversation with Rev. Ashley.

jsutton: It's the first time in a long time I haven't been obsessed over some guy to the point where I can't think straight and I start compromising. I'm learning it's okay to be unattached and it is possible for me to have a healthy friendship with a guy.

jashley: So, it's just a friendship?

jsutton: Yeah. I have a feeling Wade may want more though but I'm enjoying just being his friend. Okay, I want more too. I'm afraid of messing that up.

jashley: Have y'all actually defined your relationship?

jsutton: No, not really. We know we are attracted to each other and we have established boundaries that we have been sticking to.

Jodie heard footsteps behind her. When she checked her mirror, she saw it was just Jah-Stereo from Marketing and threw her hand up in a quick greeting. When she heard her co-workers call him Stereo, she thought it was just because of the earphones he always had on his head. It was months before she figured out it was short for Jah-Stereo, the name his mother actually gave him. Now she understood why his daughter Jacyntha's nickname is Synthesizer.

jashley: I'm so proud of you for setting boundaries! PTL! But do you think it's important to define the relationship?

jsutton: Well, I do know from experience that if something is not defined, it's easier for the lines to get blurred and you end up going somewhere you didn't mean to go.

jashley: Are you going to do something about it?

jsutton: I think Wade should initiate that. He is the man; he should take the lead. At least that's what Oneilia has always told me.

jashley: Funny, you are now choosing to follow your mom's advice. So, you are just going to wait on him?

jsutton: I'm going to let that jab go. Not exactly. I'll start praying for God's will to be done in our relationship.

Jashley: Sounds like a plan to me. Now, get back to work and I will too.

In Rev. Ashley fashion, she signed out without a formal goodbye. When she's done talking, everybody is done talking. *Just like my mama,* Jodie thought. She shook her head as she signed out and opened her spreadsheets with her client list and pending projects.

Before getting back into the groove, Jodie remembered her promise to pray. Taking to heart Rev. Longhorn's last sermon, Jodie was trying to discipline herself to pray for people and things at the time she thought about it. Pastor said that lessens the possibility that you will forget about it or change your mind. Oftentimes, we say we will pray for folks but it ends up just being lip service.

Lord, I can't thank you enough for placing Wade in my life. I thank you for his friendship, commitment, and dedication. Lord, you are in control. Please lead and guide us in the way we should go. In all things, we want you to be glorified. What is your purpose for our relationship? Is it romantic or just platonic? I pray that if there is a need for me and Wade to have a discussion about these issues that you will lay it on Wade's heart. Speak to his heart, Lord. Guide him. Give him direction and the right words to say to start the conversation. In Jesus name, I pray and receive. Amen.

~~~

Wynsome invited all the members of Truthseekers, including their newest member, Wade, and Daniel's immature suitemates, over to her parents' house for a get-together. The couple hadn't spent much time together lately and this gave Wynsome a harmless excuse to spend more time with Daniel.

She made an executive decision not to invite Rev. Ashley, though. She wanted everyone to feel comfortable talking about whatever they liked without being admonished for un-Christ-like behavior. Also, she didn't want her brother Bruce to embarrass her. He was always asking Daniel to set him up with Rev. Ashley. That was the most unlikely of a couple if there ever was one.

Wynsome had no friends to speak of to invite. These people were the only ones she spent time with outside of her family and Daniel's.

Wynsome's mom made Mexican lasagna, wedge salad, and sun tea, freshly brewed by the Alabama sun while sitting on her back porch. After dinner, the young people relaxed in the family room watching *Coming to America*. Wynsome and Bruce recited every line of the movie before it was even said. This gathering was the perfect opportunity for Bruce to ham it up, a natural-born performer.

Daniel's mind was on the conversation he needed to have with Wynsome. It had to be tonight because he had been putting it off the whole summer. Things had been extremely awkward between the two of them after the narrow escape they had that night. They had barely spent any time alone together since then. Not to mention Wynsome's attitude had turned sour and Daniel was growing increasingly distant by the day.

Brian kept making faces at Daniel to get his attention off of whatever he was thinking about but was not successful. He wanted to make him laugh or something because Daniel's solemn expression was bringing everybody down.

Jodie had been looking forward to spending time with the group. She hoped it would help her keep her mind off of Amir. Even after the terrible way he treated her, she still cared for him and missed him. She couldn't deny that Wade being in her life didn't change that.

Bruce felt the negative energy in the room and suggested they abandon the movie and go shoot pool in their parents' newly renovated basement.

Wynsome pulled Daniel to the side, hoping none of the group noticed as they filed down the steps. When they safely had the family room all to themselves, Wynsome steered him back towards the couch and snuggled up close to him. When she tried to kiss Daniel on his neck, he slid to the opposite end of the couch.

"What's wrong?" Wynsome asked.

"Wyni, there's something I've been meaning to talk to you about."

Huffing and puffing, "What about, Danny?" questioned Wynsome.

Looking down at his feet, Daniel said, ". . . about . . . my first night in the condo."

"Oh, Daniel, that happened at the beginning of the summer. If it was a problem, we should have talked about it then. I expected you to bring it up way before now, but now it's old news," Wynsome blurted out. "I know my actions must have startled you and I should not have been so forward. I'm sorry, Daniel, ok?"

Wynsome's parents peeked through the open space on the breakfast nook, wondering what all the fuss was about.

"Is everything okay?" Mr. Olivet asked. "Wynsome, you should be entertaining all your guests instead of pairing off with your boyfriend."

"Everything is fine, you guys, I just wanted to say something to Daniel in private. We will rejoin the rest of the group shortly, I promise," Wynsome explained to her parents. That seemed to be enough to satisfy them.

Reaching for Wynsome's left hand and lowering his voice, Daniel said, "It's more than just what happened that night. I am serious about waiting until marriage to have sex, and I don't think you accept that."

"Daniel, not this bull again," Wynsome sighed. She slapped his hand away and started to tap her pale pink nails on the wooden arm of the sofa. "Let's take this conversation outside."

She quickly walked to the front door with Daniel lagging behind. Once outside, she leaned on her car, wondering why Daniel was taking his precious time.

When they were safely out of earshot of her parents, they continued their conversation in the circular drive. With her arms folded in a defiant stance, Wynsome started up again, "Look, we are two grown people, and we are fully capable of deciding when it is right for us to have sex. Our decision should not be based on some antiquated customs and traditions. . ."

Standing tall, Daniel made his position clear. "Let me stop you right there. Right and wrong doesn't change with the date on the calendar. Have you even heard me over the last 12 months? I have made my decision to refrain from sex until I get married, not based on an antiquated custom or tradition. My decision is based on my relationship with Jesus, the Christ. I'm denying myself to please Him."

After a brief pause he continued, "I'm serious about this, Wyni. I love you, and I believe you are to be my wife. I want you to be my wife, but this isn't going to work if this isn't your conviction and commitment, too. You are not going to get me to change my mind. If you can't handle it, we can stop this train and you can get off now."

"After I've invested a year in this relationship, this is how it's going to end? No, it doesn't work like that," Wynsome panned.

"It doesn't have to," Daniel responded.

"No, Daniel, yeah, maybe it does. As I think about it more, I see it more clearly now. You've gotten your way for the past year. You've gotten what you wanted," Wynsome said, walking back towards the front door.

"See, it's not about me getting what I want. You don't understand Wynsome; you just don't get it! I should have known better than to get involved with a girl like you."

Turning around violently, "A girl like ME!" Wynsome shouted. What kind of girl am I, Daniel?

"A worldly girl. I was blinded by your beauty, your intellect, and your wit. And your spitfire personality, but that is what is causing all this strife. Answer me this, were you ever interested in developing a relationship with God? Or were you just waiting for a good time to turn me into your lap dog? Was I just a challenge for you? Were you even paying attention during all those worship services and Truthseekers meetings and late night conversations on the phone? When I shared my heart with you, Wyni?"

"I don't know. Let me think . . . you resort to insulting me and attacking me when things didn't work out the way you wanted them to. You asked me out!" Wynsome said with her eyes bulging and her right index finger dangerously close to his eyes.

"You knew all there was to know about me early on and now that the road is rough, you want to blame me. You can be so self-righteous! You stayed around hoping you could change me or that I would change just because you wanted me to. I think they call that 'missionary dating' in the Christian community, but what do I know, I'm just a worldly girl. Clearly, this isn't going to work, Daniel. I'm getting off the train."

Wynsome took the promise ring Daniel had given her on her birthday and threw it on the ground. Ironically, it landed in the neighbor's dog Boaz's poop. "There's your forever, ever," Wynsome declared before she went back into her parents' house and slammed the door behind her.

She didn't know what else to do. Her grief-stricken body slid down the back of the door and she sat there sobbing. At that moment, Jodie reached the landing of the stairs from the basement with her purse on her shoulder and keys in her hands, preparing to leave. Her heart melted when she saw Wynsome balled up on the floor of the foyer. Wynsome looked like how Jodie had felt not too long ago. She sat on the floor next to Wynsome and hugged her tightly from the side. Wynsome allowed her full weight to just rest on Jodie's spine.

‖‖ ‖‖ ‖‖‖

Months into Wade and Jodie's friendship, they still hadn't defined it. Jodie had been praying continuously for God's will. Wade seemed to be content with the way things were, which was strange because Jodie was sure early on he wanted more.

They still went out occasionally and frequently talked on the phone. Wade always paid, which was an added bonus. On one hand, though, it was good because her dad always taught her that's what a man should do. Apparently, none of the guys she dated in the past had been taught this. But on the other hand, it kind of confused things because Jodie didn't know whether or not to think of it as a date. She certainly was not going to ask.

Emberli kept insisting that Jodie ask Wade if he wanted a relationship with her. While Emberli had no trouble giving Jodie advice about her situation, Emberli still would not tell Jodie what was going on with her here while Jodie was in New York. Emberli stuck to her original story—she was just emotional and overreacting at the time.

Jodie no longer felt it would be inappropriate for her to broach the subject of a perceived future with Wade. It should be okay for her to ask a question she wanted the answer to, but she had a peace about leaving it alone right now.

Right when she had become completely comfortable with the way things were between the two of them, Wade decided to bring it up over an impromptu breakfast date early one Saturday morning. This time, they decided to try this little diner in the secluded Shannon area.

"You look nice, as always. You know most people just throw on some sweat pants and a wrinkled t-shirt on a Saturday morning. Not you. You manage to look fancy in jeans and a shirt," Wade pointed out.

"Thanks. I appreciate that. You give the best compliments," Jodie said blushing.

"I've had a lot on my mind lately," Wade confessed.

"What about?"

"About us. Do you think we have a future together?" Wade inquired. Taken aback, Jodie shrugged her shoulders in confusion.

Wade put it plainly, "What I'm asking is, do you want us to be exclusive and work towards marriage one day?" Again, Jodie was surprised by his candor.

Wade continued, "I think I have been in love with you ever since we met, but I became comfortable in the groove we fell into and didn't want to rock the boat. I always want to have you in my life." Jodie was elated to learn that he felt the same way she did.

"So, what are we going to do about it?" Jodie asked more so to herself.

"Well, we are both spiritually mature Christians, so I think the right answer to that question is to pray and ask God for direction," Wade said with a snide grin.

Wade was full of surprises and dropped another bomb on her that day. He suggested they take a break from each other for a couple of weeks to fast and pray. Then they would come together and share with each other what they heard from God. Jodie felt like her heart was being torn in half. She didn't want to go that long without talking to him but reluctantly, she agreed. They had to do it if God laid it on his heart.

~~~

Autumn, Jodie's favorite season, was in full bloom. She loved the sight of burnt orange, red, and yellow leaves falling off the trees and blanketing the ground. The two-lane road she took to work provided the best vista.

Jodie hardly knew what to do with herself during the time she and Wade spent fasting. The first few days were occupied by just going through the motions— morning devotion, the gym, work, church most nights, then home. She missed talking to him every morning on her ride to the office. Eventually, she realized she needed to be more proactive in seeking the Lord for direction in her relationship with Wade.

Amir also stayed on her mind constantly during that time. When she tried to study the Word, all of the few good times they had together overtook her thoughts. He even texted her to let her know he was in town for his son's twelfth birthday. She quickly deleted that message before she could even consider meeting up with him.

Jodie started doubting whether or not she had actually been delivered from that relationship. If she had, would she still be having these feelings for him? Confusion started to overtake her. Yet again, God was faithful and gave her peace that she had been delivered.

She need not forget that the devil would always try to tempt her in that area, but she had the Holy Spirit to help her to not go back down that road.

Today was a somber day, the first day after the end of Jodie and Wade's fast. Jodie couldn't even enjoy the beautiful fall landscape because she was so preoccupied with this meeting she was about to have with Wade. They decided to break the fast with a late Saturday morning breakfast at this spot in Trussville, off of Main Street. Jodie knew where all the hidden treasures of local dining were located. Most people considered her a foodie.

Wade had already found them a table in the crowded eatery. They sat and chit-chatted for the longest time, enjoying each other's company again but avoiding the subject at hand.

In frustration, Jodie blurted out, "Should I start?"

Wade laughed out of nervousness but insisted on going first.

"Jodie, you are so beautiful from the inside out. You know I enjoy your company, your zeal for the Lord, and your determination. You are definitely a woman after God's own heart."

"Thank you," Jodie said pensively

"It was hard for me to go without talking to or seeing you for fourteen days."

"Me, too."

With a nod, Wade continued, "Let me finish. On the other hand, I did gain a lot of discernment in the course of our time fasting and praying, not just about our relationship."

"Great . . .," Jodie did not know where this was going.

Wade knew what that look on her face meant. "You want me to get to the point, right?"

"Right," Jodie said. They both shared a deep throaty laugh.

"I think God is saying we should not pursue a romantic relationship, which is wild because I can't come up with any reason why not. We seem so perfect for each other."

"Really, that's what you heard from the Lord?" asked Jodie with a blank expression.

Nodding his head in the affirmative, "There is no denying the way I feel about you, but I am positive that God said you are not to be my wife."

In a low tone, Jodie responded, "I am in awe right now."

"I'm sorry; did you feel the Lord saying something different?"

Jodie paused for a long while. Her delay scared Wade. He hoped he hadn't hurt her feelings. After an equally as long sigh, she responded, "Actually, no. That is confirmation. I believe God told me the same thing. He said you are not the one He has for me."

Wade felt like he had been punched in the gut, even though he knew she was right. He resigned to the fact that things don't always turn out the way you want them to.

"You know what's funny?" Jodie said. "In the past, I've treated God's direction as more like a suggestion. I pondered it, decided if it made sense to me, and discussed it with others before I moved on it, if

191

I ever moved on it at all. I will not do that this time. I know it will be a struggle. It's more than a notion."

"I've had that problem in the past, too. I'd convince myself that's not really what God said to do," Wade added. After a long contemplative silence, Wade asked, "So, what do we do now?"

"Continue to be friends, I guess," Jodie said. "I am grateful you are a part of my life. I do not run across many young men who are for real about Jesus.

"And you are brilliant and the best sounding board ever, friend." Wade responded.

"Thank you," Jodie said. *Lord, why can't this man be for me??* "If you are not the one, God has to have someone out there for me that is even better," Jodie added trying to convince herself more than Wade.

"Umm. . . I'm not sure what to think about that comment. " Wade said.

"It's a good thing, trust me. The true test is waiting patiently on the Lord and not trying to take matters into our own hands."

After they got that out of the way, they talked about the specific things God showed Wade during the fast. He shared that God had been leading him to start a business designing webpages for area churches. He had already discussed with his pastor at Tabernacle the possibility of his home church being his first client. His pastor also gave him the names of other area pastors who may be interested. He had already put in his notice at the newspaper and planned to do the web design and freelance photography full time.

"I pray we fulfill the calling God has on both of our lives and that we both end up with the people God has designed just for us," Jodie said.

"And He continues to keep us throughout the process," Wade added.

"We shall not be idle but steady working on ourselves to be marriage material so we will be ready when God presents us with our mates," Jodie added.

"Preach, Pastor. Shut yo' mouth," Wade shouted like Deacon Odell King He wiped the imaginary sweat from his brow and threw his maple syrup soiled napkin across the small table, doing a holy dance in his seat.

"Amen," They both said in harmony, tickled.

As they walked out the restaurant and down the cobblestone sidewalk three hundred yards to their cars, Jodie remembered she needed to bring Wade up-to-date on the latest Truthseekers news.

"Oh, I forgot to tell you about Daniel and Wynsome. They broke up!"

"Really? I can't believe that."

"Yeah, when I was leaving the gathering Wynsome had at her house that night, I found her balled up crying on the floor."

"Wow. I didn't know anything like that had gone down. When she came back downstairs she looked like her regular self and told us Daniel decided to go home because he was tired."

"Wynsome is good at appearances," Jodie surmised.

"When you found her like that, did you help her or just say 'Excuse me, can I get past you. I'm leaving'", Wade asked only half-joking.

Jodie playfully punched him in the shoulder, "I sat there and cried with her. I know just how she felt. I've been there."

"Aww, somebody done made a new friend! Y'all should schedule a playdate."

"Shut up," Jodie said.

Wade elbowed her in retaliation, "For real though, I just knew Daniel would fight hard to stay with her, for better or for worse."

"I guess after a year, he realized he wasn't going to be able to make her get saved."

"She's a sweet girl when she wants to be, and I could tell she really loved Daniel, but I knew she wasn't a bit mo' interested in getting saved. What? Why you looking at me like that?" Wade asked.

Jodie just shook her head.

######### ╫╫ ╫╫ ╫╫

$\mathbf{A}$t the beginning of the New Year, Daniel still had not begged Wynsome to come back to him as she thought he would. He hadn't even called, texted, or sent an email. Wynsome was becoming more and more bitter, frustrated, and morose.

She couldn't even focus on her schoolwork to the extent that she almost failed the last semester. This was completely uncharacteristic behavior for her. Her breakup with her high school sweetheart didn't even affect her like this and he had done the unforgivable — slept with her favorite cousin who had been her best friend since birth. Their birthdays were only one day and one minute apart.

Desperate, Wynsome's parents urged her to talk to Rev. Ashley when they realized she wasn't going to let go of her pride and talk to Daniel. Rev. Ashley was relieved and full of hope when Wynsome finally reached out. She had begun to worry when Wynsome stopped responding to her phone calls and no longer attended Truthseekers. Their original group was almost non-existent, but Church had an overflow of young people to join over the summer and now they have taken over Truthseekers. Rev. Ashley no longer led the group; one of their peers did. She just showed up when she wanted to; sorta like Barbara Walters does on The View.

It was Rev. Ashley's suggestion that they meet at Salter Park around the corner from Church. Rev. Ashley often ate her lunch and had her quiet time, sitting along the man-made lake in the center of the park. Even though it was January, it was still warm and inviting in Birmingham. It was a good time to enjoy the short time that remained of this lovely weather.

They sat on a bench near the skateboard ramp and people-watched until tears suddenly started flowing down Wynsome's face. She enveloped her face in her hands trying to shield her outpour of emotion. Rev. Ashley sat there silently next to her, allowing Wynsome to get it all out. When it seemed like Wynsome had no tears left, Rev. Ashley handed her one of her church lady handkerchiefs that she always kept freshly laundered. She always had them with her for times such as these.

"So, what are the tears about?" Rev. Ashley asked in her soft voice.

With a curt tone, Wynsome answered, "I am NOT a crier, but I've been crying a lot lately, ever since me and Daniel broke up."

Staring straight ahead, Rev. Ashley asked but it came out more like a statement of fact, "The break-up has been really hard on you?"

Sniffling, Wynsome added, "I keep thinking about the last words he said to me. He called me a worldly woman. He spoke to me with such disdain. How could a guy who said he loved me say those things to me? He must have been thinking that all along."

"His approach was definitely wrong. Things don't always come out right when we say things in anger, but his words made you see how serious he was about his commitment. You know people say things they don't mean in the heat of the moment. I know Daniel genuinely loves you."

"Humph . . . Daniel is too fanatical about this religious stuff. Don't you all argue against overzealousness? What are they called—Pharisees and Sadducees? It's just not normal, Daniel is not a normal college guy. He should be out having fun and sowing his oats like my brother Bruce who is working on his second master's degree and still staying at home with my parents so his mother can do his laundry and cook his meals while he runs the streets.

You don't even seem to be as uptight as Daniel can be and you are a minister. I feel like he was trying to force his beliefs on me and I got tired of it."

"It's Pharisees," Rev. Ashley said.

"What?" Wynsome asked.

"You were talking about overzealousness. Those were the Pharisees—they were strict traditionalists. You must have picked up something at church."

"Well, I was just saying Daniel can be such a holier-than-thou nuisance."

They both watched a little white girl wander off from the other members of her group to play in a stream of water that rippled over rocks with various shapes and colors. The adults hadn't even noticed she had left the group. Rev. Ashley and Wynsome both thought they should say something but they wanted to see how long it was going to take the adults with her to notice she was missing. When the little girl's companions finally reclaimed her, Rev. Ashley spoke up.

"Did Daniel's convictions or character change any from the day you met him?"

"No."

"I know what this is really about. Your problem is not with Daniel."

"Okay. What is it about? What did the Holy Spirit show you this time?" questioned Wynsome.

"You are making jokes, but I'm serious here. The Holy Spirit is trying to get your attention. He is pulling at your heart and you are fighting it. That is what those tears are about."

"I already told you I don't understand all that super-spiritual talk. What do you mean?

"Are you starting to believe that Daniel may be on the right track? That the most important thing in life is pleasing God, being obedient to Him?"

"I don't know about that. My relationship with Daniel has been the most fulfilling relationship I've ever had. I never thought I could be so close to a guy without sleeping with him," Wynsome said, sitting straight up and turning her back to Rev. Ashley as she laid her legs on the bench with as her feet hung over the edge.

"Out of curiosity, why is having sex in a relationship so important to you?"

"I like it," Wynsome said, furrowing her brow and not understanding why Rev. Ashley asked a question with such an obvious answer. "And. . . It's the only way I know to express my feelings for a guy. I always overheard my brother on the phone telling his girlfriends that he didn't know if they really loved him unless they slept with him."

"How do you feel about that now?" Rev. Ashley asked.

"First of all, it made me lose respect for my brother. More specifically, I have learned from my relationship with Daniel that none of that is true. He is confident that I love him and that is enough for him. At least it was."

"Okay," Rev. Ashley said.

"Bruce always talked about how important it is to make sure you are compatible sexually before you marry someone. One thing Daniel said that I thought was interesting is that he believed sex was a skill. As long as we paid attention to each other's needs, we should have a great sex life and God would reward us for our obedience, anyway.

"So, you think he is right about that?"

"Yeah, I do."

Rev. Ashley chuckled, "So, are you ready to stop running from God now?"

"What makes you think I'm running?" *Did I just admit in a round-about way that I am running?* Wynsome decided to fess up, "Okay, okay. I may be running, but why should I accept Jesus? It doesn't seem to be working too well for most of the Christians I know."

"Like who?"

"Umm. . . Michelle, for one. She gave her life to Christ and died the next day. Xavier, too. He gave his life to Christ and was rewarded with a prison sentence. Let's see, Miller gave his life to Christ, but his mom is still dead, and his daddy is still in prison. Oh, and it seems like you and Jodie are destined to be single. I mean, Jodie found the perfect guy for her, but God still supposedly told her, `nope, that's not the one.' I mean, you all are not very good examples," Wynsome declared.

"Are you done?" Rev. Ashley responded.

"I think so. I've made my point."

"Good. It's time to cut the crap. You need to decide what is important to you in life. That's the bottom line."

"That's not a good defense for your team. The Christians are losing right now," Wynsome said with a smug look on her face.

"Michelle gave her life to Christ, ensuring an eternity with Him. Even though she died, many people came to Christ as a result. Many souls were saved. Maybe God decided there was more He wanted to accomplish with her death, rather than her life. The way her family rallied behind Xavier showed a lot of people what unconditional love looks like. Miller even gave his life to Christ. Now, Miller has the protection of his heavenly father while he is physically away from his earthly father."

"Umph."

"Jodie learned to love herself and accept God's love for her, instead of looking for that love in the arms of a man. You may not have Daniel, but in the process of your relationship you have come to know Christ.

"What makes you think that?"

"Again, the bottom line here is that no one is a loser. Just like the saying goes, you win some and you lose some. In these cases, the wins far outweigh the losses, which weren't really losses at all. Oftentimes,

God's prevention is God's protection. Are you ready to accept God's protection?"

"I know I have presented this hard exterior, but I know God has been working on me for the past year. I was fighting Him but I can't run any longer."

Rev. Ashley stood in agreement with Wynsome as she gave her life to Christ. She said to her, "I bet you can't wait to go tell Daniel and go get your man back!"

"I'm not running back to him. I still have my standards. He has to come get me!" Wynsome said. Rev. Ashley shook her head. *Lord, please let that be the first thing you work out in her, her pride.*